The NUTCRACKER
The Classic Christmas Fantasy

The Original Tale in Two Versions
E.T.A. Hoffmann ∞ Alexandre Dumas

FALL RIVER PRESS

Cover art by Wendy Edelson
Book design by Christine Heun

Fall River Press
122 Fifth Avenue
New York, NY 10011

ISBN: 978-1-4351-1713-6

Printed and bound in China

1 3 5 7 9 10 8 6 4 2

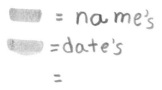

= na me's
=date's

=

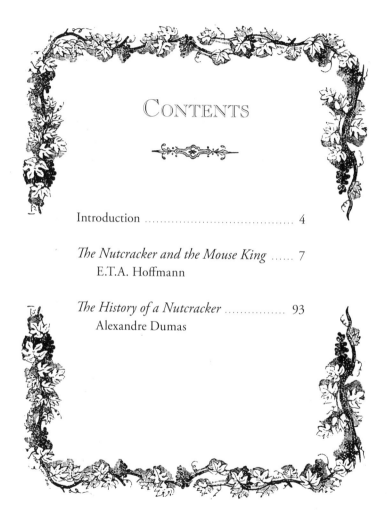

CONTENTS

Introduction

Every Christmas, millions of people young and old delight in *The Nutcracker* ballet, which tells the story of an enchanted nutcracker who one Christmas night is turned into a handsome prince through the love of a young girl, and takes her on a fantastic journey to a magical land of sweets and spices. The ballet's score, by renowned Russian composer Pyotr Ilyich Tchaikovsky, has become a beloved Christmas tradition, as recognizable as any Christmas carol or holiday song. Yet for all the popularity of this holiday confection, few people are aware that the ballet has its origins in a work of fiction written almost three-quarters of a century before its first staging, one that is very different in its telling from the story most see unfold on the ballet stage, or play on television and movie screens.

The story behind *The Nutcracker* is the creation of Ernst Theodor Amadeus Hoffmann (1776–1822), a Prussian civil servant who wrote fiction in his free time between postings that took him from Warsaw to Berlin. In his novels and stories Hoffmann, a progressive thinker, celebrated the power of art and the imagination to excite the mind and awaken the spirit. The tale of fantasy proved the perfect vehicle for what Hoffmann hoped to achieve through his writing, and his first collection of fantasies, published in 1814, earned him an appreciative audience among adult readers. Hoping similarly to reach younger readers, in 1816 Hoffman contributed two stories to a two-volume anthology of fairy tales. Among them was the tale whose title translates as "The Nutcracker and the Mouse King," which he had written for the children of his colleague and fellow civil servant Julius Hitzig.

Hoffmann later included "The Nutcracker and the Mouse King" in his four-volume compilation *The Serapion Brethren* (1819–1822). The fictional Serapions are a quartet of storytellers modeled on the literary salon that Hoffman himself presided over in Berlin, and their discussions about the interplay between the real and the imagined in the text that frames each story very probably echo those of their real-life counterparts. Lothair, the teller of "The Nutcracker and the Mouse King," defends it against his colleagues' criticisms that it will baffle younger readers, saying, "I think it is a great mistake to suppose that clever, imaginative children—and it is only they who are in question here—should content themselves with the empty nonsense which is so often set before them under the name Children's Tales. They want something much better; and it is surprising how much they see and appreciate which escapes a good, honest, well-informed papa." By including it in a book that also features tales for adults, Hoffmann clearly indicated that he did not think the story would be of interest only to children.

Credit for the widespread popularity that the story of the Nutcracker has achieved since is due largely to French author Alexandre Dumas (1802–1870), who in 1845 adapted a version of Hoffmann's tale as an entertainment for younger readers under the title *The History of a Nutcracker*. One of the bestselling writers of the nineteenth century, Dumas rendered his version of Hoffmann's tale during the same years that saw the publication of his immensely popular novels *The Three Musketeers* and *The Count of Monte Cristo*. It was translated from the French into English in 1847 as part of London book publisher Chapman and Hall's Picture Story Books series for young readers, featuring more than two hundred illustrations by Georges Bertall (reproduced throughout this edition), who had also illustrated an edition of the fairy tales of Hans Christian Anderson. It was Dumas's more precious treatment of Hoffmann's complex fairy tale that caught the eye of

Ivan Vsevolozhsky, director of Russia's Imperial Theatres, in the early 1890s. Vsevolozhsky recommended the tale to Imperial Ballet Master Marius Petipa for adaptation to the ballet stage by Tchaikovsky, and Petipa wrote the libretto to pair with Tchaikovsky's score. *The Nutcracker* debuted at the St. Petersburg Imperial Theatre in 1892. It was only a modestly popular ballet until 1954, when New York City Ballet choreographer George Balanchine presented the version that has become the standard for more than half a century.

Readers of this volume can decide for themselves which version of the story they prefer: Hoffmann's, as translated from the German by Alexander Ewing in 1892, or Dumas's, reproduced from the Chapman and Hall edition of 1847. Each presents a much fuller story than that distilled into the ballet libretto, one that includes the years-long history of the nutcracker's origins and enchantment, and an account of how it came into the possession of the enigmatic Herr Drosselmeier. Though both present a different, and sometimes darker, Nutcracker than the elegant showpiece that has come down to us from ballet stage and screen, each glimmers with the magic that has made the story, like the ballet, a classic Christmas fantasy and a timeless tale of wonder.

[*The publishers would like to thank Douglas A. Anderson and the Cotsen Children's Library of Princeton University for their invaluable assistance in the preparation of this book.*]

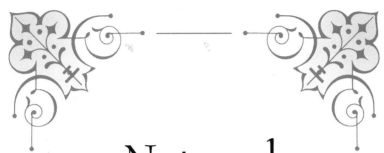

THE Nutcracker
AND THE
Mouse King

E.T.A. Hoffmann

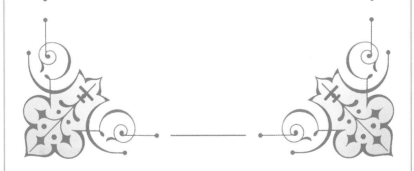

CHRISTMAS EVE

On the 24th of December Dr. Stahlbaum's children were not allowed, on any pretext whatever, at any time of all that day, to go into the small drawing-room, much less into the best drawing-room into which it opened. Fritz and Marie were sitting cowered together in a corner of the back parlour when the evening twilight fell, and they began to feel terribly eery. Seeing that no candles were brought, as was generally the case on Christmas Eve, Fritz, whispering in a mysterious fashion, confided to his young sister (who was just seven) that he had heard rattlings and rustlings going on all day, since early morning, inside the forbidden rooms, as well as distant hammerings. Further, that a short time ago a little dark-looking man had gone slipping and creeping across the floor with a big box under his arm, though he was well aware that this little man was no other than Godpapa Drosselmeier. At this news Marie clapped her little hands for gladness, and cried:

"Oh! I do wonder what pretty things Godpapa Drosselmeier has been making for us this time!"

Godpapa Drosselmeier was anything but a nice-looking man. He was little and lean, with a great many wrinkles on his face, a big patch of black plaister where his right eye ought to have been, and not a hair on his head; which was why he wore a fine white wig, made of glass, and a very beautiful work of art. But he was a very, very clever man, who even knew and understood all about clocks and watches, and could make them himself. So that when one of the beautiful clocks that were in Dr. Stahlbaum's house was out of sorts, and couldn't sing, Godpapa

Drosselmeier would come, take off his glass periwig and his little yellow coat, gird himself with a blue apron, and proceed to stick sharp-pointed instruments into the inside of the clock, in a way that made little Marie quite miserable to witness. However, this didn't really hurt the poor clock, which, on the contrary, would come to life again, and begin to whirr and sing and strike as merrily as ever; which caused everybody the greatest satisfaction. Of course, whenever he came he always brought something delightful in his pockets for the children—perhaps a little man, who would roll his eyes and make bows and scrapes, most comic to behold; or a box, out of which a little bird would jump; or something else of the kind. But for Christmas he always had some specially charming piece of ingenuity provided; something which had cost him infinite pains and labour—for which reason it was always taken away and put by with the greatest care by the children's parents.

"Oh! what can Godpapa Drosselmeier have been making for us *this* time," Marie cried, as we have said.

Fritz was of opinion that, this time, it could hardly be anything but a great castle, a fortress, where all sorts of pretty soldiers would be drilling and marching about; and then, that other soldiers would come and try to get into the fortress, upon which the soldiers inside would fire away at them, as pluckily as you please, with cannon, till every thing banged and thundered like anything.

"No, no," Marie said. "Godpapa Drosselmeier once told me about a beautiful garden, with a great lake in it, and beautiful swans swimming

about with great gold collars, singing lovely music. And then a lovely little girl comes down through the garden to the lake, and calls the swans and feeds them with shortbread and cake."

"Swans don't eat cake and shortbread," Fritz cried, rather rudely (with masculine superiority); "and Godpapa Drosselmeier couldn't make a whole garden. After all, we have got very few of his playthings; whatever he brings is always taken away from us. So I like the things papa and mamma give us much better; we keep them, all right, ourselves, and can do what we like with them."

The children went on discussing as to what he might have in store for them this time. Marie called Fritz's attention to the fact that Miss Gertrude (her biggest doll) appeared to be failing a good deal as time went on, inasmuch as she was more clumsy and awkward than ever, tumbling on to the floor every two or three minutes, a thing which did not occur without leaving very ugly marks on her face, and of course a proper condition of her clothes became out of the question altogether.

Scolding was of no use. Mamma too had laughed at her for being so delighted with Miss Gertrude's little new parasol. Fritz, again, remarked that a good fox was lacking to his small zoological collection, and that his army was quite without cavalry, as his papa was well aware. But the children knew that their elders had got all sorts of charming things ready for them, as also that the Child-Christ, at Christmas time, took special care for their wants. Marie sat in thoughtful silence, but Fritz murmured quietly to himself:

"All the same, I should like a fox and some hussars!"

It was now quite dark; Fritz and Marie sitting close together, did not dare to utter another syllable; they felt as if there were a fluttering of gentle, invisible wings around them, whilst a very far away, but unutterably beautiful strain of music could dimly be heard. Then a bright gleam of light passed quickly athwart the wall, and the children knew that the Child-Christ had sped away, on shining wings, to other happy children. At this moment a silvery bell said, "Kling-ling! Kling-ling!" the doors flew open, and such a brilliance of light came streaming from the drawing-room that the children stood rooted where they were with cries of "Oh! Oh!"

But papa and mamma came and took their hands, saying, "Come now, darlings, and see what the blessed Child-Christ has brought for you."

The Christmas Presents

I appeal to yourself, kind reader (or listener)—Fritz, Theodore, Ernest, or whatsoever your name may chance to be—and I would beg you to bring vividly before your mind's eye your last Christmas table, all glorious with its various delightful Christmas presents; and then perhaps you will be able to form some idea of the manner in which the two children stood speechless with brilliant glances fixed on all the beautiful things; how, after a little, Marie, with a sigh, cried, "Oh, how lovely! how lovely!" and Fritz gave several jumps of delight. The children had certainly been very, very good and well-behaved all the foregoing year to be thus rewarded; for never had so many beautiful and delightful things been provided for them as this time. The great Christmas tree on the table bore many apples of silver and gold, and all its branches were heavy with bud and blossom, consisting of sugar almonds, many-tinted bonbons, and all sorts of charming things to eat. Perhaps the prettiest thing about this wonder-tree, however, was the fact that in all the recesses of its spreading branches hundreds of little tapers glittered like stars, inviting the children to pluck its flowers and fruit. Also, all round the tree on every side everything shone and glittered in the loveliest manner. Oh, how many beautiful things there were! Who, oh who, could describe them all? Marie gazed there at the most delicious dolls, and all kinds of toys, and (what was the prettiest thing of all) a little silk dress with many-tinted ribbons was hung upon a projecting branch in such sort that she could admire it on all its sides; which she accordingly did, crying out several times, "Oh! the lovely, the lovely, darling little dress. And I suppose, I do believe, I shall really be allowed to put it on!" Fritz, in the meantime, had had two or three trials how his new fox (which he had actually found on the table) could gallop; and now stated that he seemed a wildish sort of brute; but, no matter, he felt sure he would soon get him well in order; and he set to work to muster his new squadron of hussars, admirably equipped, in red and gold uniforms, with real silver swords, and mounted on such shining white horses that you would have thought they were of pure silver too.

When the children had sobered down a little, and were beginning upon the beautiful picture books (which were open, so that you could see all sorts of most beautiful flowers and people of every hue, to say nothing of lovely children playing, all as naturally represented as if they were really alive and could speak), there came another tinkling of a bell, to announce the display of Godpapa Drosselmeier's Christmas present, which was on another table, against the wall, concealed by a curtain. When this curtain was drawn, what did the children behold?

On a green lawn, bright with flowers, stood a lordly castle with a great many shining windows and golden towers. A chime of bells was going on inside it; doors and windows opened, and you saw very small, but beautiful, ladies and gentlemen, with plumed hats, and long robes down to their heels, walking up and down in the rooms of it. In the central hall, which seemed all in a blaze, there were quantities of little candles burning in silver chandeliers; children, in little short doublets, were dancing to the chimes of the bells. A gentleman, in an emerald green mantle, came to a window, made signs thereat, and then disappeared inside again; also, even Godpapa Drosselmeier himself (but scarcely taller than papa's thumb) came now and then, and stood at the castle door, then went in again.

Fritz had been looking on with the rest at the beautiful castle and the people walking about and dancing in it, with his arms leant on the table; then he said:

"Godpapa Drosselmeier, let me go into your castle for a little."

Drosselmeier answered that this could not possibly be done. In which he was right; for it was silly of Fritz to want to go into a castle which was not so tall as himself, golden towers and all. And Fritz saw that this was so.

After a short time, as the ladies and gentlemen kept on walking about just in the same fashion, the children dancing, and the emerald man looking out at the same window, and Godpapa Drosselmeier coming to the door Fritz cried impatiently:

"Godpapa Drosselmeier, please come out at that other door!" "That can't be done, dear Fritz," answered Drosselmeier.

"Well," resumed Fritz, "make that green man that looks out so often walk about with the others."

"And that can't be done, either," said his godpapa, once more.

"Make the children come down, then," said Fritz. "I want to see them nearer."

"Nonsense, nothing of that sort can be done," cried Drosselmeier, with impatience. "The machinery must work as it's doing now; it can't be altered, you know."

"Oh," said Fritz, "it can't be done, eh? Very well, then, Godpapa Drosselmeier, I'll tell you what it is. If your little creatures in the castle there can only always do the same thing, they're not much worth, and

I think precious little of them! No, give me my hussars. They've got to manoeuvre backwards and forwards just as I want them, and are not fastened up in a house."

With which he made off to the other table, and set his squadron of silver horses trotting here and there, wheeling and charging and slashing right and left to his heart's content. Marie had slipped away softly, too, for she was tired of the promenading and dancing of the puppets in the castle, though, kind and gentle as she was, she did not like to show it as her brother did. Drosselmeier, somewhat annoyed, said to the parents— "After all, an ingenious piece of mechanism like this is not a matter for children, who don't understand it; I shall put my castle back in its box again." But the mother came to the rescue, and made him show her the clever machinery which moved the figures, Drosselmeier taking it all to pieces, putting it together again, and quite recovering his temper in the process. So that he gave the children all sorts of delightful brown men and women with golden faces, hands and legs, which were made of ginger cake, and with which they were greatly content.

Marie's Pet and Protégée

But there was a reason wherefore Marie found it against the grain to come away from the table where the Christmas presents were laid out; and this was, that she had just noticed a something there which she had not observed at first. Fritz's hussars having taken ground to the right at some distance from the tree, in front of which they had previously been paraded, there became visible a most delicious little man, who was standing there quiet and unobtrusive, as if waiting patiently till it should be his turn to be noticed. Objection, considerable objection, might, perhaps, have been taken to him on the score of his figure, for his body was rather too tall and stout for his legs, which were short and slight; moreover, his head was a good deal too large. But much of this was atoned for by the elegance of his costume, which showed him to be a person of taste and cultivation. He had on a very pretty violet hussar's jacket, all over knobs and braiding, pantaloons of the same, and the loveliest little boots ever seen even on a hussar officer—fitting his dear little legs just as if they had been painted on to them. It was funny, certainly, that, dressed in this style as he was, he had on a little, rather absurd, short cloak on his shoulders, which looked almost as if it were made of wood, and on his head a cap like a miner's. But Marie remembered that Godpapa Drosselmeier often appeared in a terribly ugly morning jacket, and with a frightful looking cap on his head, and yet was a very very darling godpapa.

As Marie kept looking at this little man, whom she had quite fallen in love with at first sight, she saw more and more clearly what a sweet nature and disposition was legible in his countenance. Those green eyes of his (which stuck, perhaps, a little more prominently out of his head than was quite desirable) beamed with kindliness and benevolence. It was one of his beauties, too, that his chin was set off with a well kept beard of white cotton, as this drew attention to the sweet smile which his bright red lips always expressed.

"Oh, papa, dear!" cried Marie at last, "whose is that most darling little man beside the tree?"

"Well," was the answer, "that little fellow is going to do plenty of good service for all of you; he's going to crack nuts for you, and he is to belong to Louise just as much as to you and Fritz." With which papa took him up from the table, and on his lifting the end of his wooden cloak, the little man opened his mouth wider and wider, displaying two rows of very white, sharp teeth. Marie, directed by her father, put a nut into his mouth, and—knack—he had bitten it in two, so that the shells fell down, and Marie got the kernel. So then it was explained to all that this charming little man belonged to the Nutcracker family, and was practising the profession of his ancestors. "And," said papa, "as friend Nutcracker seems to have made such an impression on you, Marie, he shall be given over to your special care and charge, though, as I said, Louise and Fritz are to have the same right to his services as you."

Marie took him into her arms at once, and made him crack some more nuts; but she picked out all the smallest, so that he might not have to open his mouth so terribly wide, because that was not nice for him. Then sister Louise came, and he had to crack some nuts for her too, which duty he seemed very glad to perform, as he kept on smiling most courteously.

Meanwhile, Fritz was a little tired, after so much drill and manoeuvring, so he joined his sisters, and laughed beyond measure at the funny little fellow, who (as Fritz wanted his share of the nuts) was passed from hand to hand, and was continually snapping his mouth open and shut. Fritz gave him all the biggest and hardest nuts he could find, but all at once there was a "crack—crack," and three teeth fell out of Nutcracker's mouth, and all his lower jaw was loose and wobbly.

"Ah! my poor darling Nutcracker," Marie cried, and took him away from Fritz.

"A nice sort of chap he is!" said Fritz. "Calls himself a

nutcracker, and can't give a decent bite—doesn't seem
to know much about his business. Hand him over
here, Marie! I'll keep him biting nuts if he drops all
the rest of his teeth, and his jaw into the bargain.
What's the good of a chap like him!"

"No, no,' said Marie, in tears; "you shan't
have him, my darling Nutcracker; see how he's
looking at me so mournfully, and showing me
his poor sore mouth. But you're a hard-hearted
creature! You beat your horses, and you've had
one of your soldiers shot."

"Those things must be done," said Fritz; "and you don't understand
anything about such matters. But Nutcracker's as much mine as yours,
so hand him over!"

Marie began to cry bitterly, and wrapped the wounded Nutcracker
quickly up in her little pocket-handkerchief. Papa and mamma came
with Drosselmeier, who took Fritz's part, to Marie's regret. But papa
said, "I have put Nutcracker in Marie's special charge, and as he seems to
have need just now of her care, she has full power over him, and nobody
else has anything to say in the matter.

And I'm surprised that Fritz
should expect further service
from a man wounded
in the execution of his
duty. As a good soldier,
he ought to know better
than that."

Fritz was much
ashamed, and, troubling
himself no further as

to nuts or nutcrackers, crept off to the other side of the table, where his hussars (having established the necessary outposts and videttes) were bivouacking for the night. Marie got Nutcracker's lost teeth together, bound a pretty white ribbon, taken from her dress, about his poor chin, and then wrapped the poor little fellow, who was looking very pale and frightened, more tenderly and carefully than before in her handkerchief. Thus she held him, rocking him like a child in her arms, as she looked at the picture-books. She grew quite angry (which was not usual with her) with Godpapa Drosselmeier because he laughed so, and kept asking how she could make such a fuss about an ugly little fellow like that. That odd and peculiar likeness to Drosselmeier, which had struck her when she saw Nutcracker at first, occurred to her mind again now, and she said, with much earnestness:

"Who knows, godpapa, if you were to be dressed the same as my darling Nutcracker, and had on the same shining boots—who knows whether you mightn't look almost as handsome as he does?"

Marie did not understand why papa and mamma laughed so heartily, nor why Godpapa Drosselmeier's nose got so red, nor why he did not join so much in the laughter as before. Probably there was some special reason for these things.

Wonderful Events

We must now explain that, in the sitting-room, on the left-hand as you go in, there stands, against the wall, a high, glass-fronted cupboard, where all the children's Christmas presents are yearly put away to be kept. Louise, the elder sister, was still quite little when her father had this cupboard constructed by a very skilful workman, who had put in it such transparent panes of glass, and altogether made the whole affair so splendid, that the things, when inside it, looked almost more shining and lovely than when one had them actually in one's hands. In the upper shelves, which were beyond the reach of Fritz and Marie, were stowed Godpapa Drosselmeier's works of art; immediately under them was the shelf for the picture-books. Fritz and Marie were allowed to do what they liked with the two lower shelves, but it always came about that the lower one of all was that in which Marie put away her dolls, as their place of residence, whilst Fritz utilized the shelf above this as cantonments for his troops of all arms. So that, on the evening as to which we are speaking, Fritz had quartered his hussars in his—the upper—shelf of these two, whilst Marie had put Miss Gertrude rather in a corner, established her new doll in the well-appointed chamber there, with all its appropriate furniture, and invited herself to tea and cakes with her. This chamber was splendidly furnished, everything on a first-rate scale, and in good and admirable style, as I have already said—and I don't know if you, my observant reader, have the satisfaction of possessing an equally well-appointed room for your dolls; a little beautifully-flowered sofa, a number of the most charming little chairs, a nice little tea-table, and, above all, a beautiful little white bed, where your pretty darling of dolls go to sleep? All this was in a corner of the shelf, the walls of which, in this part, had beautiful little pictures hanging on them; and you may well imagine that, in such a delightful chamber as this, the new doll (whose name, as Marie had discovered, was Miss Clara) thought herself extremely comfortably settled, and remarkably well off.

It was getting very late, not so very far from midnight, indeed, before the children could tear themselves away from all these Yuletide fascinations, and Godpapa Drosselmeier had been gone a considerable time. They remained riveted beside the glass cupboard, although their mother several times reminded them that it was long after bedtime. "Yes," said Fritz, "I know well enough that these poor fellows (meaning his hussars) are tired enough, and awfully anxious to turn in for the night, though as long as I'm here, not a man-jack of them dares to nod his head." With which he went off. But Marie earnestly begged for just a little while longer, saying she had such a number of things to see to, and promising that as soon as ever she had got them all settled she would go to bed at once. Marie was a very good and reasonable child, and therefore her mother allowed her to remain for a little longer with her

toys; but lest she should be too much occupied with her new doll and the other playthings so as to forget to put out the candles which were lighted all round on the wall sconces, she herself put all of them out, leaving merely the lamp which hung from the ceiling to give a soft and pleasant light. "Come soon to your bed, Marie, or you'll never be up in time in the morning," cried her mother as she went away into the bedroom.

As soon as Marie was alone, she set rapidly to work to do the thing which was chiefly at her heart to accomplish, and which, though she scarcely knew why, she somehow did not like to set about in her mother's presence. She had been holding Nutcracker, wrapped in the handkerchief, carefully in her arms all this time, and she now laid him softly down on the table, gently unrolled the handkerchief, and examined his wounds.

Nutcracker was very pale, but at the same time he was smiling with a melancholy and pathetic kindliness which went straight to Marie's heart.

"Oh, my darling little Nutcracker!" said she, very softly, "don't you be vexed because brother Fritz has hurt you so: he didn't mean it, you know; he's only a little bit hardened with his soldiering and that, but he's a good, nice boy, I can assure you: and I'll take the greatest care of you, and nurse you, till you're quite, quite better and happy again. And your teeth shall be put in again for you, and your shoulder set right; Godpapa Drosselmeier will see to that; he knows how to do things of the kind."

Marie could not finish what she was going to say, because at the mention of Godpapa Drosselmeier, friend Nutcracker made a most horrible, ugly face. A sort of green sparkle of much sharpness seemed to dart out of his eyes. This was only for an instant, however; and just

as Marie was going to be terribly frightened, she found that she was looking at the very same nice, kindly face, with the pathetic smile which she had seen before,

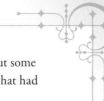

and she saw plainly that it was nothing but some draught of air making the lamp flicker that had seemed to produce the change.

"Well!" she said, "I certainly am a silly girl to be so easily frightened, and think that a wooden doll could make faces at me! But I'm too fond, really, of Nutcracker, because he's so funny, and so kind and nice; and so he must be taken the greatest care of, and properly nursed till he's quite well."

With which she took him in her arms again, approached the cupboard, and kneeling down beside it, said to her new doll: "I'm going to ask a favour of you, Miss Clara—that you will give up your bed to this poor sick, wounded Nutcracker, and make yourself as comfortable as you can on the sofa here. Remember that you're quite well and strong yourself, or you wouldn't have such fat, red cheeks, and that there are very few dolls indeed who have as comfortable a sofa as this to lie upon."

Miss Clara, in her Christmas full-dress, looked very grand and disdainful, and said not so much as "Muck!"

"Very well," said Marie, "why should I make such a fuss, and stand on any ceremony?"—took the bed and moved it forward; laid Nutcraker carefully and tenderly down on it; wrapped another pretty ribbon, taken from her own dress, about his hurt shoulder, and drew the bedclothes up to his nose.

"But he shan't stay with that nasty Clara," she said, and moved the bed, with Nutcracker in it, up to the upper shelf, so that it was placed near the village in which Fritz's hussars had their cantonments. She closed the cupboard, and was moving away to go to bed, when—listen, children!—there begun a low soft rustling and rattling, and a sort of whispering noise, all round, in all directions, from all quarters of the room—behind the stove, under the chairs, behind the cupboards. The clock on the wall "warned" louder and louder, but could not strike. Marie looked at it, and saw that the big gilt owl which was on the top of it had drooped its wings so that they covered the whole of the clock, and had stretched its cat-like head, with the crooked beak, a long way forward. And the "warning" kept growing louder and louder, with distinct words: "Clocks, clockies, stop ticking. No sound, but cautious 'warning.' Mousey king's ears are fine. Prr-prr. Only sing 'poom, poom'; sing the olden song of doom! prr-prr; poom, poom. Bells go chime! Soon rings out the fated time!" And then came "Poom! poom!" quite hoarsely and smothered, twelve times.

Marie grew terribly frightened, and was going to rush away as best she could, when she noticed that Godpapa Drosselmeier was up on the top of the clock instead of the owl, with his yellow coat-tails hanging down on both sides, like wings. But she manned herself, and called out in a loud voice of anguish:

"Godpapa! godpapa! what are you up there for? Come down to me, and don't frighten me so terribly, you naughty, naughty Godpapa Drosselmeier!"

But then there begun a sort of wild kickering and queaking, everywhere, all about, and presently there was a sound as of running and trotting, as of thousands of little feet behind the walls, and thousands of little lights began to glitter out between the chinks of the woodwork. But they were not lights; no, no! little glittering eyes; and Marie became aware that, everywhere, mice were peeping and squeezing themselves out through every chink. Presently they were trotting and galloping in all directions over the room; orderly bodies, continually increasing, of mice, forming themselves into regular troops and squadrons, in good order, just as Fritz's soldiers did when manoeuvres were going on. As Marie was not afraid of mice (as many children are), she could not help being amused by this, and her first alarm had nearly left her, when suddenly there came such a sharp and terrible piping noise that the blood ran cold in her veins. Ah! what did she see then? Well, truly, kind reader, I know that your heart is in the right place, just as much as my friend Field Marshal Fritz's is, itself, but if you had seen what now came before Marie's eyes, you would have made a clean pair of heels of it; nay, I consider that you would have plumped into your bed, and drawn the blankets further over your head than necessity demanded.

But poor Marie hadn't it in her power to do any such thing, because, right at her feet, as if impelled by some subterranean power, sand, and lime, and broken stone came bursting up, and then seven mouse-heads, with seven shining crowns upon them, rose through the floor, hissing and piping in a most horrible way. Quickly the body of the mouse which had those seven crowned heads forced its way up through the floor, and this enormous creature shouted, with its seven heads, aloud to the assembled multitude, squeaking to them with all the seven mouths in full chorus; and then the entire army set itself in motion, and went trot, trot, right up to the cupboard—and, in fact, to Marie, who was standing beside it.

Marie's heart had been beating so with terror that she had thought it must jump out of her breast, and she must die. But now it seemed to her as if the blood in her veins stood still. Half fainting, she leant backwards, and then there was a "klirr, klirr, prr," and the pane of the cupboard, which she had broken with her elbow, fell in shivers to the floor. She felt, for a moment, a sharp, stinging pain in her arm, but still, this seemed to make her heart lighter; she heard no more of the queaking and piping. Everything was quiet; and though she didn't dare to look, she thought the noise of the glass breaking had frightened the mice back to their holes.

But what came to pass then? Right behind Marie a movement seemed to commence in the cupboard, and small, feint voices began to be heard, saying:

> "Come, awake, measures take;
>   Out to the fight, out to the fight;
>   Shield the right, shield the right;
>   Arm and away, this is the night."

And harmonica-bells began ringing as prettily as you please.

"Oh! that's my little peal of bells!" cried Marie, and went nearer and looked in. Then she saw that there was bright light in the cupboard, and everything busily in motion there; dolls and little figures of various kinds all running about together, and struggling with their little arms. At this point, Nutcracker rose from his bed, cast off the bedclothes, and sprung with both feet on to the floor (of the shelf), crying out at the top of his voice:

> "Knack, knack, knack,
> Stupid mousey pack,
> All their skulls we'll crack.
> Mousey pack, knack, knack,
> Mousey pack, crick and crack,
> Cowardly lot of schnack!"

And with this he drew his little sword, waved it in the air, and cried:

"Ye, my trusty vassals, brethren and friends, are ye ready to stand by me in this great battle?"

Immediately three scaramouches, one pantaloon, four chimney-sweeps, two zither-players, and a drummer cried, in eager accents:

"Yes, your highness; we will stand by you in loyal duty; we will follow you to the death, the victory, and the fray!" And they precipitated themselves after Nutcracker (who, in the excitement of the moment, had dared that perilous leap) to the bottom shelf. Now they might well dare this perilous leap, for not only had they got plenty of clothes on, of cloth and silk, but besides, there was not much in their insides except cotton and sawdust, so that they plumped down like little wool-sacks. But as for poor Nutcracker, he would certainly have broken his arms and legs; for, bethink you, it was nearly two feet from where he had stood to the shelf below, and his body was as fragile as if he had been made of elm-wood. Yes, Nutcracker would have broken his arms and legs, had not Miss Clara started up, at the moment of his spring, from her sofa, and received the hero, drawn sword and all, in her tender arms.

"Oh! You dear, good Clara!" cried Marie, "how I did misunderstand you. I believe you were quite willing to let dear Nutcracker have your bed."

But Miss Clara now cried, as she pressed the young hero gently to her silken breast:

"Oh, my lord! Go not into this battle and danger, sick and wounded as you are. See how your trusty vassals, clowns and pantaloon, chimney-sweeps, zithermen and drummer, are already arrayed below; and the puzzle-figures, in my shelf here, are in motion, and preparing for the fray! Deign, then, oh my lord, to rest in these arms of mine, and contemplate your victory from a safe coign of vantage."

Thus spoke Clara. But Nutcracker behaved so impatiently, and kicked so with his legs, that Clara was obliged to put him down on the shelf in a hurry. However, he at once sank gracefully on one knee, and expressed himself as follows:

"Oh, lady! The kind protection and aid which you have afforded me, will ever be present to my heart, in battle and in victory!"

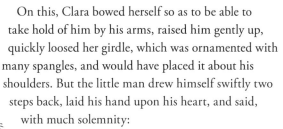

On this, Clara bowed herself so as to be able to take hold of him by his arms, raised him gently up, quickly loosed her girdle, which was ornamented with many spangles, and would have placed it about his shoulders. But the little man drew himself swiftly two steps back, laid his hand upon his heart, and said, with much solemnity:

"Oh, lady! Do not bestow this mark of your favour upon me; for—" He hesitated, gave a deep sigh, took the ribbon, with which Marie had bound him, from his shoulders, pressed it to his lips, put it on as a cognizance for the fight, and, waving his glittering sword, sprang, like a bird, over the ledge of the cupboard down to the floor.

You will observe, kind reader, that Nutcracker, even before he really came to life, had felt and understood all Marie's goodness and regard, and that it was because of his gratitude and devotion to her, that he would not take, or wear even, a ribbon of Miss Clara's, although it was exceedingly pretty and charming. This good, true-hearted Nutcracker preferred Marie's much commoner and more unpretending token.

But what is going to happen, further, now? At the moment when Nutcracker sprang down, the queaking and piping commenced again worse than ever. Alas! Under the big table, the hordes of the mouse army had taken up a position, densely massed, under the command of the terrible mouse with the seven heads. So what is to be the result?

The Battle

"Beat the Generale, trusty vassal-drummer!" cried Nutcracker, very loud; and immediately the drummer began to roll his drum in the most splendid style, so that the windows of the glass cupboard rattled and resounded. Then there began a cracking and a clattering inside, and Marie saw all the lids of the boxes in which Fritz's army was quartered bursting open, and the soldiers all came out and jumped down to the bottom shelf, where they formed up in good order. Nutcracker hurried up and down the ranks, speaking words of encouragement.

"There's not a dog of a trumpeter taking the trouble to sound a call!" he cried in a fury. Then he turned to the pantaloon (who was looking decidedly pale), and, wobbling his long chin a good deal, said, in a tone of solemnity:

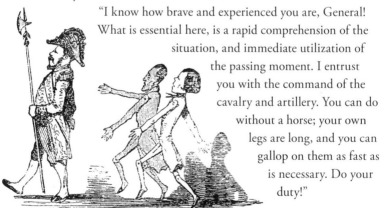

"I know how brave and experienced you are, General! What is essential here, is a rapid comprehension of the situation, and immediate utilization of the passing moment. I entrust you with the command of the cavalry and artillery. You can do without a horse; your own legs are long, and you can gallop on them as fast as is necessary. Do your duty!"

Immediately Pantaloon put his long, lean fingers to his mouth, and gave such a piercing crow that it rang as if a hundred little trumpets had been sounding lustily. Then there began a tramping and a neighing in the cupboard; and Fritz's dragoons and cuirassiers—but above all, the new glittering hussars—marched out, and then came to a halt, drawn up on the floor. They then marched past Nutcracker by regiments, with *guidons* flying and bands playing; after which they wheeled into line, and formed up at right angles to the line of march. Upon, this, Fritz's artillery came rattling up, and formed action front in advance of the halted cavalry. Then it went "boom-boom!" and Marie saw the sugar-plums doing terrible execution amongst the thickly-massed mouse-battalions, which were powdered quite white by them, and greatly put to shame. But a battery of heavy guns, which had taken up a strong position on mamma's footstool, was what did the greatest execution; and "poom-poom-poom!" kept up a murderous fire of gingerbread nuts into the enemy's ranks with most destructive effect, mowing the mice down in great numbers. The enemy, however, was not materially checked in his advance, and had even possessed himself of one or two of the heavy guns, when there came "prr-prr-prr!" and Marie could scarcely see what was happening, for smoke and dust; but this much is certain, that every corps engaged fought with the utmost bravery and determination, and it was for a long time doubtful which side would gain the day. The mice kept on developing fresh bodies of their forces, as they were advanced to the scene of action; their little silver balls—like pills in size—which they delivered with great precision (their musketry practice being specially fine) took effect even inside the glass cupboard. Clara and Gertrude ran up and down in utter despair, wringing their hands, and loudly lamenting.

"Must I—the very loveliest doll in all the world—perish miserably in the very flower of my youth?" cried Miss Clara.

"Oh! was it for this," wept Gertrude, "that I have taken such pains to *conserver* myself all these years? Must I be shot here in my own drawing-room after all?"

On this, they fell into each other's arms, and howled so terribly that you could hear them above all the din of the battle. For you have no idea of the hurly-burly that went on now, dear auditor! It went prr-prr-poof, pift-schnetterdeng—schnetterdeng—boom-booroom—boom-booroom—boom—all confusedly and higgledy-piggledy; and the mouse-king and the mice squeaked and screamed; and then again Nutcracker's powerful voice was heard shouting words of command, and issuing important orders, and he was seen striding along amongst his battalions in the thick of the fire.

Pantaloon had made several most brilliant cavalry charges, and covered himself with glory. But Fritz's hussars were subjected—by the mice—to a heavy fire of very evil-smelling shot, which made horrid spots on their red tunics; this caused them to hesitate, and hang rather back for a time. Pantaloon made them take ground to the left, in *echelon*, and, in the excitement of the moment, he, with his dragoons and cuirassiers, executed a somewhat analogous movement. That is to say, they brought up the right shoulder, wheeled to the left, and marched home to their quarters. Tins had the effect of bringing the battery of artillery on the footstool into imminent danger, and it was not long before a large body of exceedingly ugly mice delivered such a vigorous assault on this position that the whole of the footstool, with the guns and gunners, fell into the enemy's hands. Nutcracker seemed much disconcerted, and ordered his right wing to commence a retrograde movement. A soldier of your experience, my dear Fritz, knows well that such a movement is almost tantamount to a regular retreat, and you grieve, with me, in anticipation, for the disaster which threatens the army of Marie's beloved little Nutcracker. But turn your glance in the other direction, and look at this left wing of Nutcracker's, where all is still going well, and you will see that there is yet much hope for the commander-in-chief and his cause.

During the hottest part of the engagement masses of mouse-cavalry had been quietly debouching from under the chest of drawers, and had subsequently made a most determined advance upon the left wing of Nutcracker's force, uttering loud and horrible queakings. But what a reception they met with! Very slowly, as the nature of the *terrain* necessitated (for the ledge at the bottom of the cupboard had to be passed), the regiment of motto-figures, commanded by two Chinese Emperors, advanced, and formed square. These fine, brilliantly-uniformed troops, consisting of gardeners, Tyrolese, Tungooses, hairdressers, harlequins, Cupids, lions, tigers, unicorns, and monkeys, fought with the utmost courage, coolness, and steady endurance. This *bataillon d'élite* would have wrested the victory from the enemy had not one of his cavalry captains, pushing forward in a rash and foolhardy manner, made a charge upon one of the Chinese Emperors, and bitten off his head. This Chinese Emperor, in his fall, knocked over and smothered a couple of Tuugooses and a unicorn, and this created a gap, through which the enemy effected a rush, which resulted in the whole battalion being bitten to death. But the enemy gained little advantage by this; for as soon as one of the mouse-cavalry soldiers bit one of these brave adversaries to death, he found that there was a small piece of printed paper sticking in his throat, of which he died in a moment. Still, this was of small advantage to Nutcracker's army, which, having once commenced a retrograde movement, went on retreating farther and farther, suffering greater and greater loss. So that the unfortunate Nutcracker found himself driven back close to the front of the cupboard, with a very small remnant of his army.

"Bring up the reserves! Pantaloon! Scaramouch! Drummer! where the devil have you got to?" shouted Nutcracker, who was still reckoning on reinforcements from the cupboard. And there did, in fact, advance a small contingent of brown gingerbread men and women, with gilt faces, hats, and helmets; but they laid about them so clumsily that they never hit any of the enemy, and soon knocked off the cap of their commander-in-chief, Nutcracker, himself. And the enemy's chasseurs soon bit their legs off, so that they tumbled topsy-turvy, and killed several of Nutcracker's companions-in-arms into the bargain.

Nutcracker was now hard pressed, and closely hemmed in by the enemy, and in a position of extreme peril. He tried to jump the bottom ledge of the cupboard, but his legs were not long enough. Clara and Gertrude had fainted; so they could give him no assistance. Hussars and heavy

dragoons came charging up at him, and he shouted in wild despair:

"A horse! a horse! My kingdom for a horse!"

At this moment two of the enemy's riflemen seized him by his wooden cloak, and the king of the mice went rushing up to him, squeaking in triumph out of all his seven throats.

Marie could contain herself no longer. "Oh! my poor Nutcracker!" she sobbed, took her left shoe off, without very distinctly knowing what she was about, and threw it as hard as she could into the thick of the enemy, straight at their king.

Instantly everything vanished and disappeared. All was silence. Nothing to be seen. But Marie felt a more stinging pain than before in her left arm, and fell on the floor insensible.

THE INVALID

When Marie awoke from a death-like sleep she was lying in her little bed; and the sun was shining brightly in at the window, which was all covered with frost-flowers. There was a stranger gentleman sitting beside her, whom she recognized as Dr. Wendelstern. "She's awake," he said softly, and her mother came and looked at her very scrutinizingly and anxiously.

"Oh, mother!" whispered Marie, "are all those horrid mice gone away, and is Nutcracker quite safe?"

"Don't talk such nonsense, Marie," answered her mother. "What have the mice to do with Nutcracker? You're a very naughty girl, and have caused us all a great deal of anxiety. See what comes of children not doing as they're told! You were playing with your toys so late last night that you fell asleep. I don't know whether or not some mouse jumped out and frightened you, though there are no mice here, generally. But, at all events, you broke a pane of the glass cupboard with your elbow, and cut your arm so badly that Dr. Wendelstern (who has just taken a number of pieces of the glass out of your arm) thinks that if it had been only a little higher up you might have had a stiff arm for life, or even have bled to death. Thank Heaven, I awoke about twelve o'clock and missed you; and I found you lying insensible in front of the glass cupboard, bleeding frightfully, with a number of Fritz's lead soldiers scattered round you, and other toys, broken motto-figures, and gingerbread men; and Nutcracker was lying on your bleeding arm, with your left shoe not far off."

"Oh, mother, mother," said Marie, "these were the remains of the tremendous battle between the toys and the mice; and what frightened me so terribly was that the mice were going to take Nutcracker (who was the commander-in-chief of the toy army) a prisoner. Then I threw my shoe in among the mice, and after that I know nothing more that happened."

Dr. Wendelstorn gave a significant look at the mother, who said very gently to Marie:

"Never mind, dear, keep yourself quiet. The mice are all gone away, and Nutcracker's in the cupboard, quite safe and sound."

Here Marie's father came in, and had a long consultation with Dr. Wendelstern. Then he felt Marie's pulse, and she heard them talking about "wound-fever." She had to stay in bed, and take medicine, for some days, although she didn't feel at all ill, except that her arm was rather stiff and painful. She knew Nutcracker had got safe out of the battle, and she seemed to remember, as if in a dream, that he had said, quite distinctly, in a very melancholy tone:

"Marie! dearest lady! I am most deeply indebted to you. But it is in your power to do even more for me still."

She thought and thought what this could possibly be; but in vain; she couldn't make it out. She wasn't able to play on account of her arm; and when she tried to read, or look through the picture-books, everything wavered before her eyes so strangely that she was obliged to stop. So that the days seemed very long to her, and she could scarcely pass the time till evening, when her mother came and sat at her bedside, telling and reading her all sorts of nice stories. She had just finished telling her the story of Prince Fakardin, when the door opened and in came Godpapa Drosselmeier, saying:

"I've come to see with my own eyes how Marie's getting on."

When Marie saw Godpapa Drosselmeier in his little yellow coat, the scene of the night when Nutcracker lost the battle with the mice came so vividly back to her that she couldn't help crying out:

"Oh! Godpapa Drosselmeier, how nasty you were! I saw you quite well when you were sitting on the clock, covering it all over with your wings, to prevent it from striking and frightening the mice. I heard you quite well when you called the mouse-king. Why didn't you help Nutcracker? Why didn't you help me, you nasty godpapa? It's nobody's fault but yours that I'm lying here with a bad arm."

Her mother, in much alarm, asked what she meant. But Drosselmeier began making extraordinary faces, and said, in a snarling voice, like a sort of chant in monotone:

"Pendulums could only rattle—couldn't tick, ne'er a click; all the clockies stopped their ticking: no more clicking; then they all struck loud 'cling-clang.' Dollies! Don't your heads downhang! Hink and hank, and honk and hank. Doll-girls! don't your heads downhang! Cling and ring! The battle's over—Nutcracker all safe in clover. Comes the owl, on downy wing—Scares away the mouses' king. Pak and pik and pik and pook—clocks, bim-boom—grr-grr. Pendulums must click again. Tick and tack, grr and brr, prr and purr."

Marie fixed wide eyes of terror upon Godpapa Drosselmeier, because he was looking quite different, and far more horrid, than usual, and was jerking his right arm backwards and forwards as if he were some puppet moved by a handle. She was beginning to grow terribly frightened at him when her mother came in, and Fritz (who had arrived in the meantime) laughed heartily, crying, "Why, godpapa, you are going on funnily! You're just like my old Jumping Jack that I threw away last month."

But the mother looked very grave, and said, "This is a most extra-ordinary way of going on, Mr. Drosselmeier. What can you mean by it?"

"My goodness!" said Drosselmeier, laughing, "did you never hear my nice Watchmaker's Song? I always sing it to little invalids like Marie." Then he hastened to sit down beside Marie's bed, and said to her, "Don't be vexed with me because I didn't gouge out all the mouse-king's fourteen eyes. That couldn't be managed exactly; but, to make up for it, here's something which I know will please you greatly."

He dived into one of his pockets, and what he slowly, slowly brought out of it was—Nutcracker! whose teeth he had put in again quite firmly, and set his broken jaw completely to rights. Marie shouted for joy, and her mother laughed and said, "Now you see for yourself how nice Godpapa Drosselmeier is to Nutcracker."

"But you must admit, Marie," said her godpapa, "that Nutcracker is far from being what you might call a handsome fellow, and you can't say he has a pretty face. If you like I'll tell you how it was that the ugliness came into his family, and has been handed down in it from one generation to another. Did over you hear about the Princess Pirlipat, the witch Mouseyrinks, and the clever Clockmaker?"

"I say, Godpapa Drosselmeier," interrupted Fritz at this juncture, "you've put Nutcracker's teeth in again all right, and his jaw isn't wobbly as it was; but what's become of his sword? Why haven't you given him a sword?"

"Oh," cried Drosselmeier, annoyed, "you must always be bothering and finding fault with something or other, boy. What have I to do with Nutcracker's sword? I've put his mouth to rights for him; he must look out for a sword for himself."

"Yes, yes," said Fritz, "so he must, of course, if he's a right sort of fellow."

"So tell me, Marie," continued Drosselmeier, "if you know the story of Princess Pirlipat?"

"Oh no," said Marie. "Tell it me, please—do tell it me!"

"I hope it won't be as strange and terrible as your stories generally are," said her mother.

"Oh no, nothing of the kind," said Drosselmeier. "On the contrary, it's quite a funny story which I'm going to have the honour of telling this time."

"Go on then—do tell it to us," cried the children; and Drosselmeier commenced as follows:

THE STORY OF THE HARD NUT

Pirlipat's mother was a king's wife, so that, of course, she was a queen; and Pirlipat herself was a princess by birth as soon as ever she was born. The king was quite beside himself with joy over his beautiful little daughter as she lay in her cradle, and he danced round and round upon one leg, crying again and again, "Hurrah! hurrah! hip, hip, hurrah! Did anybody ever see anything so lovely as my little Pirlipat?"

And all the ministers of state, and the generals, the presidents, and the officers of the staff, danced about on one leg, as the king did, and cried as loud as they could, "No, no—never!"

Indeed, there was no denying that a lovelier baby than Princess Pirlipat was never born since the world began. Her little face looked as if it were woven of the most delicate white and rose-coloured silk; her eyes were of sparkling azure, and her hair all in little curls like threads of gold. Moreover, she had come into the world with two rows of little pearly teeth, with which, two hours after her birth, she bit the Lord High Chancellor in the fingers,
when he was making a careful examination
of her features, so that he cried, "Oh!
Gemini!" quite loud."

There are persons who
assert that "Oh Lord"
was the expression he
employed, and opinions
are still considerably
divided on this point.
At all events, she bit
him in the fingers; and
the realm learned, with

much gratification, that both intelligence and discrimination dwelt within her angelical little frame.

All was joy and gladness, as I have said, save that the queen was very anxious and uneasy, nobody could tell why. One remarkable circumstance was, that she had Pirlipat's cradle most scrupulously guarded. Not only were there lifeguardsmen always at the doors of the nursery, but—over and above the two head nurses close to the cradle—there had always to be six other nurses all round the room at night. And what seemed rather a funny thing, which nobody could understand, was that each of these six nurses had always to have a cat in her lap, and to keep on stroking it all night long, so that it might never stop purring.

It is impossible that you, my reader, should know the reason of all these precautions; but I do, and shall proceed to tell you at once.

Once upon a time, many great kings and very grand princes were assembled at Pirlipat's father's court, and very great doings were toward. Tournaments, theatricals, and state balls were going on on the grandest scale, and the king, to show that he had no lack of gold and silver, made up his mind to make a good hole in the crown revenues for once, and launch out regardless of expense. Wherefore (having previously ascertained, privately, from the state head master cook that the court astronomer had indicated a propitious hour for pork-butching), he resolved to give a grand pudding-and-sausage banquet. He jumped into a state carriage, and personally invited all the kings and the princes—to a basin of soup, merely—that he might enjoy their astonishment at the magnificence of the entertainment. Then he said to the queen, very graciously:

"My darling, *you* know exactly how I like my puddings and sausages!"

The queen quite understood what this meant. It meant that she should undertake the important duty of making the puddings and the sausages herself, which was a thing she had done on one or two previous occasions. So the chancellor of the exchequer was ordered to issue out of store the great golden sausage-kettle, and the silver *casseroles*. A great fire of sandal-wood was kindled, the queen put on her damask kitchen apron, and soon the most delicious aroma of pudding-broth rose steaming out of the kettle. This sweet smell penetrated into the very council chamber. The king could not control himself.

"Excuse me for a few minutes, my lords and gentlemen," he cried, rushed to the kitchen, embraced the queen, stirred in the kettle a little with his golden sceptre, and then went back, easier in his mind, to the council chamber.

The important juncture had now arrived when the fat had to be cut up into little square pieces, and browned on silver spits. The ladies-in-waiting retired, because the queen, from motives of love and duty to her royal consort, thought it proper to perform this important task in solitude. But when the fat began to brown, a delicate little whispering voice made itself audible, saying, "Give me some of that, sister! I want some of it, too; I am a queen as well as yourself; give me some."

The queen knew well who was speaking. It was Dame Mouseyrinks, who had been established in the palace for many years. She claimed relationship to the royal family, and she was queen of the realm of Monsolia herself, and lived with a considerable retinue of her own under the kitchen hearth. The queen was a kind-hearted, benevolent woman; and, although she didn't exactly care to recognize Dame Mouseyrinks as a sister and a queen, she was willing, at this festive season, to spare her the tit-bits she had a mind to. So she said, "Come out, then, Dame Mouseyrinks; of course you shall taste my browned fat."

So Dame Mouseyrinks came running out as fast as she could, held up her pretty little paws, and took morsel after morsel of the browned fat as the queen held them out to her. But then all Dame Mouseyrink's uncles, and

her cousins, and her aunts, came jumping out too; and her seven sons (who were terrible ne'er-do-weels) into the bargain; and they all set-to at the browned fat, and the queen was too frightened to keep them at bay. Most fortunately the mistress of the robes came in, and drove these importunate visitors away, so that a little of the browned fat was left; and this, when the court mathematician (an ex-senior wrangler of his university) was called in (which he had to be, on purpose), it was found possible, by means of skilfully devised apparatus provided with special micrometer screws, and so forth, to apportion and distribute amongst the whole of the sausages, &c., under construction.

The kettledrums and the trumpets summoned all the great princes and potentates to the feast. They assembled in their robes of state; some of them on white palfreys, some in crystal coaches. The king received them with much gracious ceremony, and took his seat at the head of the table, with his crown on, and his sceptre in his hand. Even during the serving of the white pudding course, it was observed that he turned pale, and raised his eyes to heaven; sighs heaved his bosom; some terrible inward pain was clearly raging within him. But when the black-puddings were handed round, he fell back in his seat, loudly sobbing and groaning.

Every one rose from the table, and the court physician tried in vain to feel his pulse. Ultimately, after the administration of most powerful remedies—burnt feathers, and the like—his majesty

seemed to recover his senses to some extent, and stammered, scarce audibly, the words: "Too little fat!"

The queen cast herself down at his feet in despair, and cried, in a voice broken by sobs, "Oh, my poor unfortunate royal consort! Ah, what tortures you are doomed to endure! But see the culprit here at your feet Punish her severely! Alas! Dame Mouseyrinks, her uncles, her seven sons, her cousins and her aunts, came and ate up nearly all the fat—and—"

Here the queen fell back insensible.

But the king jumped up, all anger, and cried in a terrible voice, "Mistress of the robes, what is the meaning of this?"

The mistress of the robes told all she knew, and the king resolved to take revenge on Dame Mouseyrinks and her family for eating up the fat which ought to have been in the sausages. The privy council was summoned, and it was resolved that Dame Mouseyrinks should be tried for her life, and all her property confiscated. But as his majesty was of opinion that she might go on consuming the fat, which was his appanage, the whole matter was referred to the court

Clockmaker and Arcanist—whose name was the same as mine—Christian Elias Drosselmeier, and he undertook to expel Dame Mouseyrlinks and all her relations from the palace precincts forever, by means of a certain politico-diplomatic procedure. He invented certain ingenious little machines, into which pieces of browned fat were inserted; and he placed these machines down all about the dwelling of Dame Mouseyrinks. Now she herself was much too knowing not to see through Drosselmeier's artifice; but all her remonstrances and warnings to her relations were unavailing. Enticed by the fragrant odour of the browned fat, all her seven sons, and a great many of her uncles, her cousins and her aunts, walked into Drosselmeier's little machines, and were immediately taken prisoners by the fall of a small grating; after which they met with a shameful death in the kitchen.

Dame Mouseyrinks left this scene of horror with her small following. Rage and despair filled her breast. The court rejoiced greatly; the queen was very anxious, because she knew Dame Mouseyrinks' character, and knew well that she would never allow

the death of her sons and other relatives to go unavenged. And, in fact, one day when the queen was cooking a fricassee of sheep's lights for the king (a dish to which he was exceedingly partial), Dame Mouseyrinks suddenly made her appearance, and said: "My sons and my uncles, my cousins and my aunts, are now no more. Have a care, lady, lest the queen of the mice bites your little princess in two! Have a care!"

With which she vanished, and was no more seen. But the queen was so frightened that she dropped the fricassee into the fire; so this was the second time Dame Mouseyrinks spoiled one of the king's favourite dishes, at which he was very irate.

* * * * *

But this is enough for to-night; we'll go on with the rest of it another time.

Sorely as Marie—who had ideas of her own about this story—begged Godpapa Drosselmeier to go on with it, he would not be persuaded, but jumped up, saying, "Too much at a time wouldn't be good for you; the rest tomorrow."

Just as Drosselmeier was going out of the door, Fritz said : "I say, Godpapa Drosselmeier, was it really you who invented mousetraps?"

"How can you ask such silly questions?" cried his mother. But Drosselmeier laughed oddly, and said: "Well, you know I'm a clever clockmaker. Mousetraps had to be invented some time or other."

* * * * *

And now you know, children (said Godpapa Drosselmeier the next evening) why it was the queen took such precautions about her little Pirlipat. Had she not always the fear before her eyes of Dame Mouseyrinks coming back and carrying out her threat of biting the princess to death? Drosselmeier's ingenious machines were of no avail against the clever, crafty Dame Mouseyrinks, and

nobody save the court astronomer, who was also state astrologer and reader of the stars, knew that the family of the Cat Purr had the power to keep her at bay. This was the reason why each of the lady nurses was obliged to keep one of the sons of that family (each of whom was given the honorary rank and title of "privy councillor of legation") in her lap, and render his onerous duty less irksome by gently scratching his back.

One night, just after midnight, one of the chief nurses stationed close to the cradle, woke suddenly from a profound sleep. Everything lay buried in slumber. Not a purr to be heard—deep, deathlike silence, so that the death-watch ticking in the wainscot sounded quite loud. What were the feelings of this principal nurse when she saw, close beside her, a great, hideous mouse, standing on its hind legs, with its horrid head laid on the princess's face! She sprang up with a scream of terror. Everybody awoke; but then Dame Mouseyrinks (for she was the great big mouse in Pirlipat's cradle) ran quickly away into the corner of the room. The privy councillors of legation dashed after her, but too late! She was off and away through a chink in the floor. The noise awoke Pirlipat, who cried terribly. "Heaven be thanked, she is still alive!" cried all the nurses; but what was their horror when they looked at Pirlipat, and saw what the beautiful, delicate little thing had turned into. An enormous bloated head (instead of the pretty little golden-haired one), at the top of a diminutive, crumpled-up body, and green, wooden-looking eyes staring, where the lovely azure-blue pair had been, whilst her mouth had stretched across from the one ear to the other.

Of course the queen nearly died of weeping and loud lamentation, and the walls of the king's study

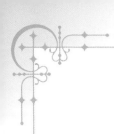

had all to be hung with padded arras, because he kept on banging his head against them, crying:

"Oh! wretched king that I am! Oh, wretched king that I am!"

Of course he might have seen, then, that it would have been much better to eat his puddings with no fat in them at all, and let Dame Mouseyrinks and her folk stay on under the hearthstone. But Pirlipat's royal father thought not of that. What he did was to lay all the blame on the court Clockmaker and Arcanist, Christian Elias Drosselmeier, of Nürnberg. Wherefore he promulgated a sapient edict to the effect that said Drosselmeier should, within the space of four weeks, restore Princess Pirlipat to her pristine condition—or, at least, indicate an

unmistakable and reliable process whereby that might be accomplished—or else suffer a shameful death by the axe of the common headsman.

Drosselmeier was not a little alarmed; but he soon began to place confidence in his art, and in his luck; so he proceeded to execute the first operation which seemed to him to be expedient. He took Princess Pirlipat very carefully to pieces, screwed off her hands and her feet, and examined her interior structure. Unfortunately, he found

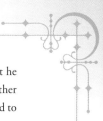

that the bigger she got the more deformed she would be, so that he didn't see what was to be done at all. He put her carefully together again, and sank down beside her cradle—which he wasn't allowed to go away from—in the deepest dejection.

The fourth week had come, and Wednesday of the fourth week, when the king came in, with eyes gleaming with anger, made threatening gestures with his sceptre, and cried:

"Christian Elias Drosselmeier, restore the princess, or prepare for death!"

Drosselmeier began to weep bitterly. The little princess kept on cracking nuts, an occupation which seemed to afford her much quiet satisfaction. For the first time the Arcanist was struck by Pirlipat's remarkable appetite for nuts, and the circumstance that she had been born with teeth. And the fact had been that immediately after her transformation she had begun to cry, and she had gone on crying till by chance she got hold of a nut. She at once cracked it, and ate the

kernel, after which she was quite quiet. From that time her nurses found that nothing would do but to go on giving her nuts.

"Oh, holy instinct of nature—eternal, mysterious, inscrutable Interdependence of Things!" cried Drosselmeier, "thou pointest out to me the door of the secret. I will knock, and it shall be opened unto me."

He at once begged for an interview with the Court Astronomer, and was conducted to him closely guarded. They embraced, with many tears, for they were great friends, and then retired into a private closet, where they referred to many books treating of sympathies, antipathies, and other mysterious subjects. Night came on. The Court Astronomer consulted the stars, and, with the assistance of Drosselmeier (himself an adept in astrology), drew the princess's horoscope. This was an exceedingly difficult operation, for the lines kept getting more and more entangled and confused for ever so long. But at last—oh what joy!—it lay plain before them that all the princess had to do to be delivered from the enchantment which made her so hideous, and get back her former beauty, was to eat the sweet kernel of the nut Crackatook.

Now this nut Crackatook had a shell so hard that you might have fired a forty-eight pounder at it without producing the slightest effect on it. Moreover, it was essential that this nut should be cracked, in the princess's presence, by the teeth of a man whose beard had never known a razor, and who had never had on boots. This man had to hand the kernel to her with his eyes closed, and he might not open them till he had made seven steps backwards without a stumble.

Drosselmeier and the astronomer had been at work on this problem uninterruptedly for three days and three nights; and on the Saturday the king was sitting at dinner, when Drosselmeier—who was to have been beheaded on the Sunday morning—burst joyfully in to announce that he had found out what had to be done to restore Princess Pirlipat to her pristine beauty. The king embraced him in a burst of rapture, and promised him a diamond sword, four decorations, and two Sunday suits.

"Set to work immediately after dinner," the monarch cried: adding, kindly, "Take care, dear Arcanist, that the young unshaven gentleman in shoes, with the nut Crackatook all ready in his hand, is on the spot; and be sure that he touches no liquor beforehand, so that he mayn't trip up when he makes his seven backward steps like a crab. He can get as drunk as a lord afterwards, if he likes."

Drosselmeier was dismayed at this utterance of the king's, and stammered out, not without trembling and hesitation, that, though the remedy was discovered, both the nut Crackatook and the young gentleman who was to crack it had still to be searched for, and that it was matter of doubt whether they ever would be got hold of at all. The king, greatly incensed, whirled his sceptre round his crowned head, and shouted, in the voice of a lion:

"Very well, then you must be beheaded!"

It was exceedingly fortunate for the wretched Drosselmeier that the king had thoroughly enjoyed his dinner that day, and was consequently in an admirable temper, and disposed to listen to the sensible advice which the queen, who was very sorry for Drosselmeier, did not spare to give him. Drosselmeier took heart, and represented that he really had fulfilled the conditions, and discovered the necessary measures, and had gained his life, consequently. The king said this was all bosh and nonsense; but at length, after two or three glasses of liqueurs, decreed that Drosselmeier and the astronomer should start off immediately, and not come back without the nut Crackatook in their pockets. The man who was to crack it (by the queen's suggestion) might be heard of by means of advertisements in the local and foreign newspapers and gazettes.

* * * * *

Godpapa Drosselmeier interrupted his story at this point, and promised to finish it on the following evening.

Next evening, as soon as the lights were brought, Godpapa Drosselmeier duly arrived, and went on with his story as follows:

* * * * *

Drosselmeier and the court astronomer had been journeying for fifteen long years without finding the slightest trace of the nut Crackatook. I might go on for more than four weeks telling you where all they had been, and what extraordinary things they had seen. I shall not do so, however, but merely mention that Drosselmeier, in his profound discouragement, at last began to feel a most powerful longing to see his dear native town of Nürnberg once again. And he was more powerfully moved by this longing than usual one day, when he happened to be smoking a pipe of kanaster with his friend in the middle of a great forest in Asia, and he cried:

"Oh, Nürnberg, Nürnberg! dear native town—he who still knows thee not, place of renown—though far he has travelled, and great cities seen—as London, and Paris, and Peterwardeen—knoweth not what it is happy to be—still must his longing heart languish for thee—for thee, O Nürnberg, exquisite town—where the houses have windows both upstairs and down!"

As Drosselmeier lamented thus dolefully, the astronomer, seized with compassionate sympathy, began to weep and howl so terribly that he was heard throughout the length and breadth of Asia. But he collected himself again, wiped the tears from his eyes, and said:

"After all, dearest colleague, why should we sit and weep and howl here? Why not come to Nürnberg? Does it matter a brass farthing, after all, where and how we search for this horrible nut Crackatook?"

"That's true, too," answered Drosselmeier, consoled. They both got up immediately, knocked the ashes out of their pipes, started off, and travelled straight on without stopping, from that forest right in the centre of Asia till they came to Nürnberg. As soon as they got there, Drosselmeier went straight to his cousin the toymaker and doll-carver, and gilder and varnisher, whom he had not seen for a great many long years. To him he told all the tale of Princess Pirlipat, Dame Mouseyrinks, and the nut Crackatook, so that he clapped his hands repeatedly, and cried in amazement:

"Dear me, cousin, these things are really wonderful—very wonderful, indeed!"

Drosselmeier told him, further, some of the adventures he had met with on his long journey—how he had spent two years at the court of the King of Dates; how the Prince of Almonds had expelled him with ignominy from his territory; how he had applied in vain to the Natural History Society at Squirreltown—in short, how he had been everywhere utterly unsuccessful in discovering the faintest trace of the nut Crackatook. During this narrative, Christoph Zacharias had kept frequently snapping his fingers, twisting himself round on one foot, smacking with his tongue, etc.; then he cried:

"Ee—aye—oh!—that really would be the very deuce and all."

At last he threw his hat and wig in the air, warmly embraced his cousin, and cried:

"Cousin, cousin, you're a made man—a made man you are—
for either I am much deceived, or I have got the nut Crackatook
myself!"

He immediately produced a little cardboard box, out of which he
took a gilded nut of medium size.

"Look there!" he said, showing this nut to his cousin; "the state
of matters as regards this nut is this. Several years ago, at Christmas
time, a stranger man came here with a sack of nuts, which he offered
for sale. Just in front of my shop he got into a quarrel, and put the
sack down the better to defend himself from the nut-sellers of the
place, who attacked him. Just then a heavily-loaded waggon drove

over the sack, and all the nuts were
smashed but one. The stranger
man, with an odd smile, offered
to sell me this nut for a twenty-

kreuzer piece of the year 1796. This struck me as strange. I found just such a coin in my pocket, so I bought the nut, and I gilt it over, though I didn't know why I took the trouble quite, or should have given so much for it."

All question as to its being really the long-sought nut Crackatook was dispelled when the Court Astronomer carefully scraped away the gilding, and found the word "Crackatook" graven on the shell in Chinese characters.

The joy of the exiles was great, as you may imagine; and the cousin was even happier, for Drosselmeier assured him that he was a made man too, as he was sure of a good pension, and all the gold leaf he would want for the rest of his life for his gilding, free, gratis, for nothing.

The Arcanist and the Astronomer had both got on their nightcaps, and were going to turn into bed, when the astronomer said:

"I tell you what it is, dear colleague, one piece of good fortune never comes alone. I feel convinced that we've not only found the nut, but the young gentleman who is to crack it, and hand the beauty-restoring kernel to the princess, into the bargain. I mean none other than your cousin's son here, and I don't intend to close an eye this night till I've drawn that youngster's horoscope."

With which he threw away his nightcap, and at once set to work to consult the stars. The cousin's son was a nice-looking, well-grown young fellow, had never been shaved, and had never worn boots. True, he had been a Jumping Jack for a Christmas or two in his earlier days, but there was scarcely any trace of this discoverable about him, his appearance had been so altered by his father's care. He had appeared last Christmas in a beautiful red coat with gold trimmings, a sword by his side, his hat under his arm, and a fine wig with a pigtail. Thus apparelled, he stood in his father's shop exceeding lovely to behold, and from his native *galanterie* he occupied himself in cracking nuts for the young ladies, who called him "the handsome nutcracker."

Next morning the Astronomer fell, with much emotion, into the Arcanist's arms, crying:

"This is the very man!—we have got him!—he is found! Only, dearest colleague, two things we must keep carefully in view. In the first place, we must construct a most substantial pigtail for this precious nephew of yours, which shall be connected with his lower jaw in such sort that it shall be capable of communicating a very powerful pull to it. And next, when we get back to the Residenz, we must carefully conceal the fact that we have brought the young gentleman who is to shiver the nut back with us. He must not make his appearance for a considerable time after us. I read in the horoscope that if two or three others bite at the nut unsuccessfully to begin with, the king will promise the man who breaks it—and, as a consequence, restores the princess her good looks—the princess's hand and the succession to the crown."

The doll-maker cousin was immensely delighted with the idea of his son's marrying Princess Pirlipat, and being a prince and king, so he gave him wholly over to the envoys to do what they liked with him. The pigtail which Drosselmeier attached to him proved to be a very powerful and efficient instrument, as he exemplified by cracking the hardest of peach-stones with the utmost ease.

Drosselmeier and the Astronomer, having at once sent the news to the Residenz of the discovery of the nut Crackatook, the necessary advertisements were at once put in the newspapers, and, by the time that our travellers got there, several nice young gentlemen, among whom there were princes even, had arrived, having sufficient confidence in their teeth to try to disenchant the princess. The ambassadors were horrified when they saw poor Pirlipat again. The diminutive body with tiny hands and feet was not big enough to support the great shapeless head. The hideousness of the face was enhanced by a beard like white cotton, which had grown about the mouth and chin. Everything had turned out as the court astronomer had read it in the horoscope. One milksop in shoes after another bit his teeth and his jaws into agonies over the nut, without doing the princess the slightest good in the world. And then, when he was carried out on the verge of insensibility by the dentists who were in attendance on purpose, he would sigh:

"Ah dear, that was a hard nut."

Now when the king, in the anguish of his soul, had promised to him who should disenchant the princess his daughter and the kingdom, the charming, gentle young Drosselmeier made his appearance, and begged to be allowed to make an attempt. None of the previous ones had pleased the princess so much. She pressed her little hands to her heart and sighed:

"Ah, I hope it will be he who will crack the nut, and be my husband."

When he had politely saluted the king, the queen, and the Princess Pirlipat, he received the nut Crackatook from the hands of the Clerk of the Closet, put it between his teeth, made a strong effort with his head, and—crack—crack—the shell was shattered into a number of pieces. He neatly cleared the kernel from the pieces of husk which were sticking to it, and, making a leg, presented it courteously to the princess, after which he closed his eyes and began his backward steps. The princess swallowed the kernel, and—oh marvel!—the monstrosity vanished, and in its place there stood a wonderfully beautiful lady, with a face which seemed woven of delicate lily-white and rose-red silk, eyes of sparkling azure, and hair all in little curls like threads of gold.

Trumpets and kettledrums mingled in the loud rejoicings of the populace. The king and all his court danced about on one leg, as they had done at Pirlipat's birth, and the queen had to be treated with Eau de Cologne, having fallen into a fainting fit from joy and delight. All this tremendous tumult interfered not a little with young Drosselmeier's self-possession, for he still had to make his seven backward steps. But he collected himself as best he could, and was just stretching out his right foot to make his seventh step, when up came Dame Mouseyrinks through the floor, making a horrible weaking and squeaking, so that Drosselmeier, as he was putting his foot down, trod upon her, and stumbled so that he almost fell. Oh misery!— all in an instant he was transmogrified, just as the princess had been before: his body all shrivelled up, and could scarcely support the great shapeless head with enormous projecting eyes, and the wide gaping mouth. In the place where his pigtail used to be a scanty wooden cloak hung down, controlling the movements of his nether jaw.

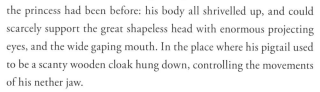

The clockmaker and the astronomer were wild with terror and consternation, but they saw that Dame Mouseyrinks was wallowing in her gore on the floor. Her wickedness had not escaped punishment, for young Drosselmeier had squashed her so in the throat with the sharp point of his shoe that she was mortally hurt.

But as Dame Mouseyrinks lay in her death agony she queaked and cheeped in a lamentable style, and cried:

"Oh, Crackatook, thou nut so hard!—Oh, fate, which none may disregard!—Hee hee, pee pee, woe's me, I cry!—since I through that hard nut must die.—But, brave young

Nutcracker, I see—you soon must follow after me.—My sweet young son, with sevenfold crown—will soon bring Master Cracker down.—His mother's death he will repay—so, Nutcracker, beware that day!—Oh, life most sweet, I feebly cry—I leave you now, for I must die. Queak!"

With this cry died Dame Mouseyrinks, and her body was carried out by the Court Stovelighter. Meantime nobody had been troubling themselves about young Drosselmeier. But the princess reminded the king of his promise, and he at once directed that the young hero should be conducted to his presence. But when the poor wretch came forward in his transmogrified condition the princess put both her hands to her face, and cried:

"Oh please take away that horrid Nutcracker!"

So that the Lord Chamberlain seized him immediately by his little shoulders, and shied him out at the door. The king, furious at the idea of a nutcracker being brought before him as a son-in-law, laid all the blame upon the clockmaker and the astronomer, and ordered them both to be banished for ever.

The horoscope which the astronomer had drawn in Nürnberg had said nothing about this; but that didn't hinder him from taking some fresh observations. And the stars told him that young Drosselmeier would conduct himself so admirably in his new condition that he would yet be a prince and a king, in spite of his transmogrification; but also that his deformity would only disappear after the son of Dame Mouseyrinks, the seven-headed king of the mice (whom she had born after the death of her original seven sons) should perish by his hand, and a lady should fall in love with him notwithstanding his deformity.

That is the story of the hard nut, children, and now you know why people so often use the expression "that was a hard nut," and why Nutcrackers are so ugly.

* * * * *

Thus did Godpapa Drosselmeier finish his tale. Marie thought the Princess Pirlipat was a nasty ungrateful thing. Fritz, on the other hand, was of opinion that if Nutcracker had been a proper sort of fellow he would soon have settled the mouse king's hash, and got his good looks back again.

UNCLE AND NEPHEW

Should any of my respected readers or listeners ever have happened to be cut by glass they will know what an exceedingly nasty thing it is, and how long it takes to get well. Marie was obliged to stay in bed a whole week, because she felt so terribly giddy whenever she tried to stand up; but at last she was quite well again, and able to jump about as of old. Things in the glass cupboard looked very fine indeed—everything new and shiny, trees and flowers and houses—toys of every kind. Above all, Marie found her dear Nutcracker again, smiling at her in the second shelf, with his teeth all sound and right. As she looked at this pet of hers with much fondness, it suddenly struck her that all Godpapa Drosselmeier's story had been about Nutcracker, and his family feud with Dame Mouseyrinks and her people. And now she knew that her Nutcracker was none other than young Mr. Drosselmeier, of Nürnberg, Godpapa Drosselmeier's delightful nephew, unfortunately under the spells of Dame Mouseyrinks. For whilst the story was being told, Marie couldn't doubt for a moment that the clever clockmaker at Pirlipat's father's court was Godpapa Drosselmeier himself.

"But why didn't your uncle help you? Why didn't he help you?" Marie cried, sorrowfully, as she felt more and more clearly every moment that in the battle, which she had witnessed, the question in dispute had been no less a matter than Nutcracker's crown and kingdom. Weren't all the other toys his subjects? And wasn't it clear that the astronomer's prophecy that he was to be rightful King of Toyland had come true?

Whilst the clever Marie was weighing all these things in her mind, she kept expecting that Nutcracker and his vassals would give some indications of being alive, and make some movements as she looked at them. This, however, was by no means the case. Everything in the cupboard kept quite motionless and still. Marie thought this was the effect of Dame Mouseyrinks's enchantments, and those of her seven-headed son, which still were keeping up their power.

"But," she said, "though you're not able to move, or to say the least little word to me, dear Mr. Drosselmeier, I know you understand me, and see how very well I wish you. Always reckon on my assistance when you require it. At all events, I will ask your uncle to aid you with all his great skill and talents, whenever there may be an opportunity."

Nutcracker still kept quiet and motionless. But Marie fancied that a gentle sigh came breathing through the glass cupboard, which made its panes ring in a wonderful, though all but imperceptible, manner—whilst something like a little bell-toned voice seemed to sing:

"Marie fine, angel mine! I will be thine, if thou wilt be mine!"

Although a sort of cold shiver ran through her at this, still it caused her the keenest pleasure.

Twilight came on. Marie's father came in with Godpapa Drosselmeier, and presently Louise set out the tea-table, and the family took their places round it, talking in the pleasantest and merriest manner about all sorts of things. Marie had taken her little stool, and sat down at her godpapa's feet in silence. When everybody happened to cease talking at the same time, Marie looked her godpapa full in the face with her great blue eyes, and said:

"I know now, godpapa, that my Nutcracker is your nephew, young Mr. Drosselmeier from Nürnberg. The prophecy has come true: he is a king and a prince, just as your friend the astronomer said he would be. But you know as well as I do that he is at war with Dame Mouseyrink's son—that horrid king of the mice. Why don't you help him?"

Marie told the whole story of the battle, as she had witnessed it, and was frequently interrupted by the loud laughter of her mother and sister; but Fritz and Drosselmeier listened quite gravely.

"Where in the name of goodness has the child got her head filled with all that nonsense?" cried her father.

"She has such a lively imagination, you see," said her mother; "she dreamt it all when she was feverish with her arm."

"It is all nonsense," cried Fritz, 'and it isn't true! my red hussars are not such cowards as all that. If they were, do you suppose I should command them?"

But godpapa smiled strangely, and took little Marie on his knee, speaking more gently to her than ever he had been known to do before.

"More is given to you, Marie dear," he said, "than to me, or the others. You are a born princess, like Pirlipat, and reign in a bright beautiful country. But you still have much to suffer, if you mean to befriend poor transformed Nutcracker; for the king of the mice lies in wait for him at every turn. But I cannot help him; you, and you only, can do that. So be faithful and true."

Neither Marie nor any of the others knew what Godpapa Drosselmeier meant by these words. But they struck Dr. Stahlbaum—the father—as being so strange that he felt Drosselmeier's pulse, and said:

"There seems a good deal of congestion about the head, my dear sir. I'll just write you a little prescription."

But Marie's mother shook her head meditatively, and said:

"I have a strong idea what Mr. Drosselmeier means, though I can't exactly put it in words."

Victory

It was not very long before Marie was awakened one bright moonlight night by a curious noise, which came from one of the corners of her room. There was a sound as of small stones being thrown, and rolled here and there; and between whiles came a horrid cheeping and squeaking.

"Oh, dear me! here come these abominable mice again!" cried Marie, in terror, and she would have awakened her mother. But the noise suddenly ceased; and she could not move a muscle—for she saw the king of the mice working himself out through a hole in the wall; and at last he came into the room, ran about in it, and got on to the little table at her bed-head with a great jump.

"Hee-hehee!" he cried; "give me your sweetmeats! out with your cakes, marchpane and sugar-stick, gingerbread cakes! Don't pause to argue! If yield them you won't, I'll chew up Nutcracker! See if I don't!"

As he cried out these terrible words he gnashed and chattered his teeth most frightfully, and then made off again through the hole in the wall. This frightened Marie so that she was quite pale in the morning, and so upset that she scarcely could utter a word. A hundred times she felt impelled to tell her mother or her sister, or at all events her brother, what had happened. But she thought, "of course none of them would believe me. They would only laugh at me."

But she saw well enough that to succour Nutcracker she would have to sacrifice all her sweet things; so she laid out all she had of them at the bottom of the cupboard next evening.

"I can't make out how the mice have got into the sitting-room," said her mother. "This is something quite new. There never were any there before. See, Marie, they've eaten up all your sweetmeats."

And so it was: the epicure mouse king hadn't found the marchpane altogether to his taste, but had gnawed all round the edges of it, so that what he had left of it had to be thrown into the ash-pit. Marie never minded about her sweetmeats, being delighted to think that she had saved Nutcracker by means of them. But what were her feelings when next night there came a queaking again close by her ear. Alas! The king of the mice was there again, with his eyes glaring worse than the night before.

"Give me your sugar toys," he cried; "give them you must, or else I'll chew Nutcracker up into dust!"

Then he was gone again.

Marie was very sorry. She had as beautiful a collection of sugar-toys as ever a little girl could boast of. Not only had she a charming little shepherd, with his shepherdess, looking after a flock of milk-white sheep, with a nice dog jumping about them, but two postmen with letters in their hands, and four couples of prettily dressed young gentlemen and most beautifully dressed young ladies, swinging in a Russian swing. Then there were two or three dancers, and behind them Farmer Feldkuemmel and the Maid of Orleans. Marie didn't much care about them; but back in the corner there was a little baby with red cheeks, and this was Marie's darling. The tears came to her eyes.

"Ah!" she cried, turning to Nutcracker, "I really will do all I can to help you. But it's very hard."

Nutcracker looked at her so piteously that she determined to sacrifice everything—for she remembered the mouse king with all his seven

mouths wide open to swallow the poor young fellow; so that night she
set down all her sugar figures in front of the cupboard, as she had the
sweetmeats the night before. She kissed the shepherd, the shepherdess,
and the lambs; and at last she brought her best beloved of all, the little
red-cheeked baby from its corner, but did put it a little further back than
the rest. Farmer Feldkuemmel and the Maid of Orleans had to stand in
the front rank of all.

"This is really getting too bad," said Marie's mother the next morning;
"some nasty mouse or other must have made a hole in the glass cupboard,
for poor Marie's sugar figures are all eaten and gnawed." Marie really
could not restrain her tears. But she was soon able to smile again; for she
thought, "What does it matter? Nutcracker is safe."

In the evening Marie's mother was telling her father and Godpapa
Drosselmeier about the mischief which some mouse was doing in the
children's cupboard, and her father said:

"It's a regular nuisance! What a pity it is that we can't get rid of it. It's
destroying all the poor child's things."

Fritz intervened, and remarked:

"The baker downstairs has a fine grey
Councillor-of-Legation; I'll go and get
hold of him, and he'll soon put a stop
to it, and bite the mouse's head off,
even if it's Dame Mouseyrinks herself,
or her son, the king of the mice."

"Oh, yes!" said his mother,
laughing, "and jump up on to
the chairs and tables, knock
down the cups and glasses,
and do ever so much mischief
besides."

"No, no!" answered Fritz; "the baker's Councillor-of-Legation's a very clever fellow. I wish I could walk about on the edge of the roof, as he does."

"Don't let us have a nasty cat in the house in the night-time," said Louise, who hated cats.

"Fritz is quite right though," said the mother; "unless we set a trap. Haven't we got such a thing in the house?"

"Godpapa Drosselmeier's the man to get us one," said Fritz; "it was he who invented them, you know." Everybody laughed. And when the mother said they did not possess such a thing, Drosselmeier said he had plenty; and he actually sent a very fine one round that day. When the cook was browning the fat, Marie—with her head full of the marvels of her godpapa's tale—called out to her:

"Ah, take care, Queen! Remember Dame Mouseyrinks and her people." But Fritz drew his sword, and cried, "Let them come if they dare! I'll give an account of them." But everything about the hearth remained quiet and undisturbed. As Drosselmeier was fixing the browned fat on a fine thread, and setting the trap gently down in the glass cupboard, Fritz cried:

"Now, Godpapa Clockmaker, mind that the mouse king doesn't play you some trick!"

Ah, how did it fare with Marie that night? Something as cold as ice went tripping about on her arm, and something rough and nasty laid itself on her cheek, and cheeped and queaked in her ear. The horrible mouse king came and sat on her shoulder, foamed a blood-red foam out of all his seven mouths, and chattering and grinding his teeth, he hissed into Marie's ear:

"Hiss, hiss!—keep away—don't go in there—ware of that house—don't you be caught—death to the mouse—hand out your picture-books—none of your scornful looks!—Give me your dresses—also your laces—or, if you don't, leave you I won't—Nutcracker I'll bite—drag him out of your sight—his last hour is near—so tremble for fear!—Fee, fa, fo, fum—his last hour is come!—Hee hee, pee pee—queak—queak!"

Marie was overwhelmed with anguish and sorrow, and was looking quite pale and upset when her mother said to her next morning:

"This horrid mouse hasn't been caught. But never mind, dear, we'll catch the nasty thing yet, never fear. If the traps won't do, Fritz shall fetch the grey Councillor of Legation."

As soon as Marie was alone, she went up to the glass cupboard, and said to Nutcracker, in a voice broken by sobs:

"Ah, my dear, good Mr. Drosselmeier, what can I do for you, poor unfortunate girl that I am! Even if I give that horrid king of the mice all my picture-books, and my new dress which the Child Christ gave me at Christmas as well, he's sure to go on asking for more; so I soon shan't have anything more left, and he'll want to eat me! Oh, poor thing that I am! What shall I do? What shall I do?"

As she was thus crying and lamenting, she noticed that a great spot of blood had been left, since the eventful night of the battle, upon Nutcracker's neck. Since she had known that he was really young Mr. Drosselmeier, her godpapa's nephew, she had given up carrying him in her arms, and petting and kissing him; indeed, she felt a delicacy about touching him at all. But now she took him carefully out of his shelf, and began to wipe off this blood-spot with her handkerchief. What were her feelings when she found that Nutcracker was growing warmer and warmer in her hand, and beginning to move! She put him back into the cupboard as fast as she could. His mouth began to wobble backwards and forwards, and he began to whisper, with much difficulty:

"Ah, dearest Miss Stahlbaum—most precious of friends! How deeply I am indebted to you for everything—for everything! But don't, don't sacrifice any of your picture-books or pretty dresses for me. Get me a sword—a sword is what I want. If you get me that, I'll manage the rest—though—he may—"

There Nutcracker's speech died away, and his eyes, which had been expressing the most sympathetic grief, grew staring and lifeless again.

Marie felt no fear; she jumped for joy, rather, now that she knew how to help Nutcracker without further painful sacrifices. But where on earth was she to get hold of a sword for him? She resolved to take counsel with Fritz; and that evening, when their father and mother had gone out, and they two were sitting beside the glass cupboard, she told him what had passed between her and Nutcracker with the king of the mice, and what it was that was required to rescue Nutcracker.

The thing which chiefly exercised Fritz's mind was Marie's statement as to the unexemplary conduct of his red hussars in the great battle. He asked her once more, most seriously, to assure him if it really was the truth; and when she had repeated her statement, on her word of honour, he advanced to the cupboard, and made his hussars a most affecting address; and, as a punishment for their behaviour, he solemnly took their plumes one by one out of their busbies, and prohibited them from sounding the march of the hussars of the guard for the space of a twelvemonth. When he had performed this duty, he turned to Marie, and said:

"As far as the sword is concerned, I have it in my power to assist Nutcracker. I placed an old Colonel of Cuirassiers on retirement on a pension, no longer ago than yesterday, so that he has no further occasion for his sabre, which is sharp."

This Colonel was settled, on his pension, in the back corner of the third shelf. He was fetched out from thence, and his sabre—still a bright and handsome silver weapon—taken off, and girt about Nutcracker.

Next night Marie could not close an eye for anxiety. About midnight she fancied she heard a strange stirring and noise in the sitting-room—a rustling and a clanging—and all at once came a shrill "Queak!"

"The king of the mice! The king of the mice!" she cried, and jumped out of bed, all terror. Everything was silent; but soon there came a gentle tapping at the door of her room, and a soft voice made itself heard, saying:

"Please to open your door, dearest Miss Stahlbaum! Don't be in the least degree alarmed; good, happy news!"

It was Drosselmeier's voice—young Drosselmeier's, I mean. She threw on her dressing-gown, and opened the door as quickly as possible. There stood Nutcracker, with his sword, all covered with blood, in his right hand, and a little wax taper in his left. When he saw Marie he knelt down on one knee, and said:

"It was you, and you only, dearest lady, who inspired me with knightly valour, and steeled me with strength to do battle with the insolent caitiff who dared to insult you. The treacherous king of the mice lies vanquished and writhing in his gore! Deign, lady, to accept these tokens of victory from the hand of him who is, till death, your true and faithful knight."

With this Nutcracker took from his left arm the seven crowns of the mouse king, which he had ranged upon it, and handed them to Marie, who received them with the keenest pleasure. Nutcracker rose, and continued as follows:

"Oh! My best beloved Miss Stahlbaum, if you would only take the trouble to follow me for a few steps, what glorious and beautiful things I could show you, at this supreme moment when I have overcome my hereditary foe! Do—do come with me, dearest lady!"

TOYLAND

I feel quite convinced, children, that none of you would have hesitated for a moment to go with good, kind Nutcracker, who had always shown himself to be such a charming person, and Marie was all the more disposed to do as he asked her, because she knew what her just claims on his gratitude were, and was sure that he would keep his word, and show her all sorts of beautiful things. So she said:

"I will go with you, dear Mr. Drosselmeier; but it mustn't be very far, and it won't do to be very long, because, you know, I haven't had any sleep yet."

"Then we will go by the shortest route," said Nutcracker, "although it is, perhaps, rather the most difficult."

He went on in front, followed by Marie, till he stopped before the big old wardrobe. Marie was surprised to see that, though it was generally shut, the doors of it were now wide open, so that she could see her father's travelling cloak of fox-fur hanging in the front. Nutcracker clambered deftly up this cloak, by the edgings and trimmings of it, so as to get hold of the big tassel which was fastened at the back of it by a thick cord. He gave this tassel a tug, and a pretty little ladder of cedar-wood let itself quickly down through one of the arm-holes of the cloak.

"Now, Miss Stahlbaum, step up that ladder, if you will be so kind," said Nutcracker. Marie did so. But as soon as she had got up through the arm-hole, and begun to look out at the neck, all at once a dazzling light came streaming on to her, and she found herself standing on a lovely, sweet-scented meadow, from which millions of sparks were streaming upward, like the glitter of beautiful gems.

"This is Candy Mead, where we are now," said Nutcracker. "But we'll go in at that gate there."

Marie looked up and saw a beautiful gateway on the meadow, only a few steps off. It seemed to be made of white, brown, and raisin-coloured marble; but when she came close to it she saw it was all of baked sugar-almonds and raisins, which—as Nutcracker said when they were going through it—was the reason it was called "Almond and Raisin Gate." There was a gallery running round the upper part of it, apparently made of barley-sugar, and in this gallery six monkeys, dressed in red doublets, were playing on brass instruments in the most delightful manner ever heard; so that it was all that Marie could do to notice that she was walking along upon a beautiful variegated marble pavement, which, however, was really a mosaic of lozenges of all colours. Presently the sweetest of odours came breathing round her, streaming from a beautiful little wood on both sides of the way. There was such a glittering and sparkling among the dark foliage, that one could see all the gold and silver fruits hanging on the many-tinted stems, and these stems and branches were all ornamented and dressed up in ribbons and bunches of flowers, like brides and bridegrooms, and festive wedding guests. And as the orange perfume came wafted, as if on the wings of gentle zephyrs, there was a soughing among the leaves and branches, and all the gold-leaf and tinsel rustled and tinkled like beautiful music, to which the sparkling lights could not help dancing.

"Oh, how charming this is!" cried Marie, enraptured.

"This is Christmas Wood, dearest Miss Stahlbaum," said Nutcracker.

"Ah!" said Marie, "if I could only stay here for a little! Oh, it is so lovely!"

Nutcracker clapped his little hands, and immediately there appeared a number of little shepherds and shepherdesses, and hunters and huntresses, so white and delicate that you would have thought they were made of pure sugar, whom Marie had not noticed before, although they had been walking about in the wood: and they brought a beautiful gold reclining chair, laid down a white satin cushion in it, and politely invited Marie to take a seat. As soon as she did so, the shepherds and shepherdesses danced a pretty ballet, to which the hunters and huntresses played the music on their horns, and then they all disappeared amongst the thickets.

"I must really apologize for the poor style in which this dance was executed, dearest Miss Stahlbaum," said Nutcracker. "These people all belong to our Wire Ballet Troupe, and can only do the same thing over and over again. Had we not better go on a little farther?"

"Oh, I'm sure it was all most delightful, and I enjoyed it immensely!" said Marie, as she stood up and followed Nutcracker, who was going on leading the way. They went by the side of a gently rippling brook, which seemed to be what was giving out all the perfume which filled the wood.

"This is Orange Brook," said Nutcracker; "but, except for its sweet scent, it is nothing like as fine a water as the River Lemonade, a beautiful broad stream, which falls—as this one does also—into the Almond-milk Sea."

And, indeed, Marie soon heard a louder plashing and rushing, and came in sight of the River Lemonade, which went rolling along in swelling waves of a yellowish colour, between banks covered with a herbage and underwood which shone like green carbuncles. A remarkable freshness and coolness, strengthening heart and breast, exhaled from this fine river. Not far from it a dark yellow stream crept sluggishly along, giving out a most delicious odour; and on its banks sat numbers of pretty children, angling for little fat fishes, which they ate as soon as they caught them. These fish were very much like filberts, Marie saw when she came closer. A short distance farther, on the banks of this stream, stood a nice little village. The houses of this village, and the church, the parsonage, the barns, and so forth, were all dark brown with gilt roofs, and many of the walls looked as if they were plastered over with lemon-peel and shelled almonds.

"That is Gingerthorpe on the Honey River," said Nutcracker. "It is famed for the good looks of its inhabitants; but they are very short-tempered people, because they suffer so much from tooth-ache. So we won't go there at present."

At this moment Marie caught sight of a little town where the houses were all sorts of colours and quite transparent, exceedingly pretty to look at. Nutcracker went on towards this town, and Marie heard a noise of bustle and merriment, and saw some thousands of nice little folks unloading a number of waggons which were drawn up in the market-place. What they were unloading from the waggons looked like packages of coloured paper, and tablets of chocolate.

"This is Bonbonville," Nutcracker said. "An embassy has just arrived from Paperland and the King of Chocolate. These poor Bonbonville people have been vexatiously threatened lately by the Fly-Admiral's forces, so they are covering their houses over with their presents from Paperland, and constructing fortifications with the fine pieces of workmanship which the Chocolate-King has sent them. But oh! dearest Miss Stahlbaum, we are not going to restrict ourselves to seeing the small towns and villages of this country. Let us be off to the metropolis."

He stepped quickly onwards, and Marie followed him, all expectation. Soon a beautiful rosy vapour began to rise, suffusing everything with a soft splendour. She saw that this was reflected from a rose-red, shining water, which went plashing and rushing away in front of them in wavelets of roseate silver. And on this delightful water, which kept broadening and broadening out wider and wider, like a great lake, the loveliest swans were floating, white as silver, with collars of gold. And, as if vieing with each other, they were singing the most beautiful songs, at which little fish, glittering like diamonds, danced up and down in the rosy ripples.

"Oh!" cried Marie, in the greatest delight, "this must be the lake which Godpapa Drosselmeier was once going to make for me, and I am the girl who is to play with the swans."

Nutcracker gave a sneering sort of laugh, such as she had never seen in him before, and said:

"My uncle could never make a thing of this kind. You would be much more likely to do it yourself. But don't let us bother about that. Rather let us go sailing over the water, Lake Rosa here, to the metropolis."

The Metropolis

Nutcracker clapped his little hands again, and the waves of Lake Rosa began to sound louder and to plash higher, and Marie became aware of a sort of car approaching from the distance, made wholly of glittering precious stones of every colour, and drawn by two dolphins with scales of gold. Twelve of the dearest little negro boys, with head-dresses and doublets made of humming-birds' feathers woven together, jumped to land, and carried first Marie and then Nutcracker, gently gliding above the water, into the car, which immediately began to move along over the lake of its own accord. Ah! how beautiful it was when Marie went onward thus over the waters in the shell-shaped car, with the rose-perfume breathing around her, and the rosy waves plashing. The two golden-scaled dolphins lifted their nostrils, and sent streams of crystal high in the air; and as these fell down in glittering, sparkling rainbows, there was a sound as of two delicate, silvery voices, singing, "Who comes over the rosy sea?—Fairy is she. Bim-bim—fishes; sim-sim—swans; sfa-sfa—golden birds; tratrah, rosy waves, wake you, and sing, sparkle and ring, sprinkle and kling—this is the fairy we languish to see—coming at last to us over the sea. Rosy waves dash—bright dolphins play—merrily, merrily on!"

But the twelve little black boys at the back of the car seemed to take some umbrage at this song of the water-jets; for they shook the sun-shades they were holding so that the palm leaves they were made of clattered and rattled together; and as they shook them they stamped an odd sort of rhythm with their feet, and sang:

"Klapp and klipp, and klipp and klapp, and up and down."

"Negroes are merry, amusing fellows," said Nutcracker, a little put out; "but they'll set the whole lake into a state of regular mutiny on my hands!" And in fact there did begin a confused, and confusing, noise of strange voices which seemed to be floating both in the water and in the air. However, Marie paid no attention to it, but went on looking into the perfumed rosy waves, from each of which a pretty girl's face smiled back to her.

"Oh! look at Princess Pirlipat," she cried, clapping her hands with gladness, "smiling at me so charmingly down there! Do look at her, Mr. Drosselmeier."

But Nutcracker sighed, almost sorrowfully, and said: "That is not Princess Pirlipat, dearest Miss Stahlbaum, it is only yourself; always your own lovely face smiling up from the rosy waves."

At this Marie drew her head quickly back, closed her eyes as tightly as she could, and was terribly ashamed. But just then the twelve negroes lifted her out of the car and set her on shore. She found herself in a small thicket or grove, almost more beautiful even than Christmas Wood, everything glittered and sparkled so in it. And the fruit on the trees was extraordinarily wonderful and beautiful, and not only of very curious colours, but with the most delicious perfume.

"Ah!" said Nutcracker, "here we are in Comfit Grove, and yonder lies the metropolis."

How shall I set about describing all the wonderful and beautiful sights which Marie now saw, or give any idea of the splendour and magnificence of the city which lay stretched out before her on a flowery plain? Not only did the walls and towers of it shine in the brightest and most gorgeous colours, but the shapes and appearance of the buildings were like nothing to be seen on earth. Instead of roofs the houses had on beautiful twining crowns, and the towers were garlanded with beautiful leaf-work, sculptured and carved into exquisite, intricate designs. As they passed in at the gateway, which looked as if it was made entirely of macaroons and sugared fruits, silver soldiers presented arms, and a little man in a brocade

dressing-gown threw himself upon Nutcracker's neck, crying:

"Welcome, dearest prince! welcome to Sweetmeatburgh!"

Marie wondered not a little to see such a very grand personage recognise young Mr. Drosselmeier as a prince. But she heard such a number of small delicate voices making such a loud clamouring and talking, and such a laughing and chattering going on, and such a singing and playing, that she couldn't give her attention to anything else, but asked Drosselmeier what was the meaning of it all.

"Oh, it is nothing out of the common, dearest Miss Stahlbaum," he answered. "Sweetmeatburgh is a large, populous city, full of mirth and entertainment. This is only the usual thing that is always going on here every day. Please to come on a little farther."

After a few paces more they were in the great marketplace, which presented the most magnificent appearance. All the houses which were round it were of filagreed sugar-work, with galleries towering above galleries; and in the centre stood a lofty cake covered with sugar, by way of obelisk, with fountains round it spouting orangeade, lemonade, and other delicious beverages into the air. The runnels at the sides of the footways were full of creams, which you might have ladled up with a spoon if you had chosen. But prettier than all this were the delightful little people who were crowding about everywhere by the thousand, shouting, laughing, playing, and singing, in short, producing all that jubilant uproar which Marie had heard from the distance. There were beautifully dressed ladies and gentlemen, Greeks and Armenians, Tyrolese and Jews, officers and soldiers, clergymen, shepherds, jack-puddings, in short, people of every conceivable kind to be found in the world.

The tumult grew greater towards one of the corners; the people streamed asunder. For the Great Mogul happened to be passing along there in his palanquin, attended by three-and-ninety grandees of the realm, and seven hundred slaves. But it chanced that the Fishermen's Guild, about five hundred strong, were keeping a festival at the opposite corner of the place; and it was rather an unfortunate coincidence that the Grand Turk took it in his head just at this particular moment to go out for a ride, and crossed the square with three thousand Janissaries. And, as if this were not enough, the grand procession of the Interrupted Sacrifice came along at the same time, marching up towards the obelisk with a full orchestra playing, and the chorus singing:

"Hail! all hail to the glorious sun!"

So there was a thronging and a shoving, a driving and a squeaking; and soon lamentations arose, and cries of pain, for one of the fishermen had knocked a Brahmin's head off in the throng, and the Great Mogul had been very nearly run down by a jack-pudding. The din grew wilder and wilder. People were beginning to shove one another, and even to come to fisticuffs; when the man in the brocade dressing-gown who had welcomed Nutcracker as prince at the gate, clambered up to the top of the obelisk, and, after a very clear-tinkling bell had rung thrice, shouted, very loudly, three several times:

"Pastrycook! pastrycook! pastrycook!"

Instantly the tumult subsided. Everybody tried to save his bacon as quickly as he could; and, after the entangled processions had been got disentangled, the dirt properly brushed off the Great Mogul, and the Brahmin's head stuck on again all right, the merry noise went on just the same as before.

"Tell me why that gentleman called out 'Pastrycook,' Mr. Drosselmeier, please," said Marie.

"Ah! dearest Miss Stahlbaum," said Nutcracker, "in this place 'Pastrycook' means a certain unknown and very terrible Power, which, it is believed, can do with people just what it chooses. It represents the Fate, or Destiny, which rules these happy little people, and they stand in such awe and terror of it that the mere mention of its name quells the wildest tumult in a moment, as the burgomaster has just shown. Nobody thinks further of earthly matters, cuffs in the ribs, broken heads, or the like. Every one retires within himself, and says:

"What is man? and what his ultimate destiny?"

Marie could not forbear a cry of admiration and utmost astonishment as she now found herself all of a sudden before a castle, shining in roseate radiance, with a hundred beautiful towers. Here and there at intervals upon its walls were rich bouquets of violets, narcissus, tulips, carnations, whose dark, glowing colours heightened the dazzling whiteness, inclining to rose-colour, of the walls. The great dome of the central building, as well as the pyramidal roofs of the towers, were set all over with thousands of sparkling gold and silver stars.

"Aha!" said Nutcracker, "here we are at Marchpane Castle at last!"

Marie was sunk and absorbed in contemplation of this magic palace. But the fact did not escape her that the roof was wanting to one of the principal towers, and that little men, up upon a scaffold made of sticks of cinnamon, were busy putting it on again. But before she had had time to ask Nutcracker about this, he said:

"This beautiful castle was a short time since threatened with tremendous havoc, if not with total destruction. Sweet-tooth the giant happened to be passing by, and he bit off the top of that tower there, and was beginning to gnaw at the great dome. But the Sweetmeatburgh people brought him a whole quarter of the town by way of tribute, and a considerable slice of Comfit Grove into the bargain. This stopped his mouth, and he went on his way."

At this moment soft, beautiful music was heard, and out came twelve little pages with lighted clove-sticks, which they held in their little hands by way of torches. Each of their heads was a pearl, their bodies were emeralds and rubies, and their feet were beautifully-worked pure gold. After them came four ladies about the size of Marie's Miss Clara, but so gloriously and brilliantly attired that Marie saw in a moment that they could be nothing but princesses of the blood royal. They embraced Nutcracker most tenderly, and shed tears of gladness, saying:

"Oh, dearest prince! beloved brother!"

Nutcracker seemed deeply affected. He wiped away his tears, which flowed thick and fast, and then he took Marie by the hand and said, with much pathos and solemnity:

"This is Miss Marie Stahlbaum, the daughter of a most worthy medical man, and the preserver of my life. Had she not thrown her slipper just in the nick of time—had she not procured me the pensioned Colonel's sword—I should have been lying in my cold grave at this moment, bitten to death by the accursed king of the mice. I ask you to tell me candidly, can Princess Pirlipat, princess though she be, compare for a moment with Miss Stahlbaum here in beauty, in goodness, in virtues of every kind? My answer is, emphatically 'No.' "

All the ladies cried "No"; and they fell upon Marie's neck with sobs and tears, and cried: "Ah! noble preserver of our beloved royal brother! Excellent Miss Stahlbaum!"

They now conducted Marie and Nutcracker into the castle, to a hall whose walls were composed of sparkling crystal. But what delighted Marie most of all was the furniture. There were the most darling little chairs, bureaus, writing-tables, and so forth, standing about everywhere, all made of cedar or Brazil-wood, covered with golden flowers. The princesses made Marie and Nutcracker sit down, and said that they would themselves prepare a banquet. So they went and brought quantities of little cups and dishes of the finest Japanese porcelain, and spoons, knives and forks,

graters and stew- pans, and other kitchen utensils of gold and silver. Then they fetched the most delightful fruits and sugar things—such as Marie had never seen the like of—and began to squeeze the fruit in the daintiest way with their little hands, and to grate the spices and rub down the sugar-almonds; in short, they set to work so skilfully that Marie could see very well how accomplished they were in kitchen matters, and what a magnificent banquet there was going to be. Knowing her own skill in this line, she wished, in her secret heart, that she might be allowed to go and help the princesses, and have a finger in all these pies herself. And the prettiest of Nutcracker's sisters, just as if she had read the wishes of Marie's heart, handed her a little gold mortar, saying:

"Sweet friend, dear preserver of my brother, would you mind just pounding a little of this sugar-candy?"

Now as Marie went on pounding in the mortar with good will and the utmost enjoyment—and the sound of it was like a lovely song—Nutcracker began to relate, with much minuteness and prolixity, all that had happened on the occasion of the terrible engagement between his forces and the army of the king of the mice; how he had had the worst of it on account of the bad behaviour of his troops; how the horrible mouse king had all but bitten him to death, so that Marie had had to sacrifice a number of his subjects who were in her service, etc., etc.

During all this it seemed to Marie as if what Nutcracker was saying—and even the sound of her own mortar—kept growing more and more indistinct, and going farther and farther away. Presently she saw a silver mistiness rising up all about, like clouds, in which the princesses, the pages, Nutcracker, and she herself were floating. And a curious singing and a buzzing and humming began, which seemed to die away in the distance; and then she seemed to be going up—up—up, as if on waves constantly rising and swelling higher and higher, higher and higher, higher and higher.

Conclusion

And then came a "prr-poof," and Marie fell down from some inconceivable height.

"That was a crash and a tumble!"

However, she opened her eyes, and, lo and behold, there she was in her own bed! It was broad daylight, and her mother was standing at her bedside, saying:

"Well, what a sleep you have had! Breakfast has been ready for ever so long."

Of course, dear audience, you see how it was. Marie, confounded and amazed by all the wonderful things she had seen, had fallen asleep at last in Marchpane Castle, and the negroes or the pages, or perhaps the princesses themselves, had carried her home and put her to bed.

"Oh, mother darling," said Marie, "what a number of places young Mr. Drosselmeier has taken me to in the night, and what beautiful things I have seen!" And she gave very much the same faithful account of it all as I have done to you.

Her mother listened, looking at her with much astonishment, and, when she had finished, said:

"You have had a long, beautiful dream, Marie; but now you must put it all out of your head."

Marie firmly maintained that she had not been dreaming at all; so her mother took her to the glass cupboard, lifted out Nutcracker from his usual position on the third shelf, and said:

"You silly girl, how can you believe that this wooden figure can have life and motion?"

"Ah, mother," answered Marie, "I know perfectly well that Nutcracker is young Mr. Drosselmeier from Nürnberg, Godpapa Drosselmeier's nephew."

Her father and mother both burst out into ringing laughter.

"It's all very well your laughing at poor Nutcracker, father," cried Mary, almost weeping; "but he spoke very highly of you; for when we arrived at Marchpane Castle, and he was introducing me to his sisters, the princesses, he said you were a most worthy medical man."

The laughter grew louder, and Louise, and even Fritz, joined in it. Marie ran into the next room, took the mouse king's seven crowns from her little box, and handed them to her mother, saying:

"Look there, then, dear mother; those are the mouse king's seven crowns which young Mr. Drosselmeier gave me last night as a proof that he had got the victory."

Her mother gazed in amazement at the little crowns, which were made of some very brilliant, wholly unknown metal, and worked more beautifully than any human hands could have worked them. Dr. Stahlbaum could not cease looking at them with admiration and astonishment either, and both the father and the mother enjoined Marie most earnestly to tell them where she really had got them from. But she could only repeat what she had said before; and when her father scolded her, and accused her of untruthfulness, she began to cry bitterly, and said:

"Oh, dear me; what can I tell you except the truth, poor unfortunate girl that I am!"

At this moment the door opened, and Godpapa Drosselmeier came in, crying:

"Hullo! hullo! What's all this? My little Marie crying? What's all this? what's all this?"

Dr. Stahlbaum told him all about it, and showed him the crowns. As soon as he had looked at them, however, he cried out:

"Stuff and nonsense! stuff and nonsense! These are the crowns I used to wear on my watch-chain. I gave them as a present to Marie on her second birthday. Do you mean to tell me you don't remember?"

None of them did remember anything of the kind. But Marie, seeing that her father and mother's faces were clear of clouds again, ran up to her godpapa, crying:

"You know all about the affair, Godpapa Drosselmeier; tell it to them then. Let them know from your own lips that my Nutcracker is your nephew, young Mr. Drosselmeier from Nürnberg, and that it was he who gave me the crowns."

But Drosselmeier made a very angry face, and muttered, "Stupid stuff and nonsense!" upon which Marie's father took her in front of him, and said, with much earnestness:

"Now just look here, Marie; let there be an end of all this foolish trash and absurd nonsense for once and for all; I'm not going to allow any more of it; and if ever I hear you say again that that idiotic, misshapen Nutcracker is your godpapa's nephew, I shall shy, not only Nutcracker, but all your other playthings—Miss Clara not excepted—out of the window."

Of course poor Marie dared not utter another word concerning that which her whole mind was full of, for you may well suppose that it was impossible for anyone

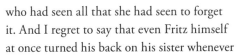

who had seen all that she had seen to forget it. And I regret to say that even Fritz himself at once turned his back on his sister whenever she wanted to talk to him about the wondrous realm in which she had been so happy. Indeed, he is said to have frequently murmured, "Stupid goose!" between his teeth, though I can scarcely think this compatible with his proved kindness of heart. This much, however, is matter of certainty, that, as he no longer believed what his sister said, he now, on a public parade, formally recanted what he had said to his red hussars, and, in the place of the plumes he had deprived them of, gave them much taller and finer ones of goose quills, and allowed them to sound the march of the hussars of the guard as before.

Marie did not dare to say anything more of her adventures. But the memories of that fairy realm haunted her with a sweet intoxication, and the music of that delightful, happy country still rang sweetly in her ears. Whenever she allowed her thoughts to dwell on all those glories she saw them again, and so it came about that, instead of playing as she used to do, she sat quiet and meditative, absorbed within herself. Everybody found fault with her for being this sort of little dreamer.

It chanced one day that Godpapa Drosselmeier was repairing one of the clocks in the house, and Marie was sitting beside the glass cupboard, sunk in her dreams and gazing at Nutcracker. All at once she said, as if involuntarily:

"Ah, dear Mr. Drosselmeier, if you really were alive, I shouldn't be like Princess Pirlipat, and despise you because you had had to give up being a nice handsome gentleman for my sake!"

"Stupid stuff and nonsense!" cried Godpapa Drosselmeier.

But, as he spoke, there came such a tremendous bang and shock that Marie fell from her chair insensible.

When she came back to her senses her mother was busied about her and said:

"How could you go and tumble off your chair in that way, a big girl like you? Here is Godpapa Drosselmeier's nephew come from Nürnberg. See how good you can be."

Marie looked up. Her godpapa had got on his yellow coat and his glass wig, and was smiling in the highest good-humour. By the hand he was holding a very small but very handsome young gentleman. His little face was red and white; he had on a beautiful red coat trimmed with gold lace, white silk stockings and shoes, with a lovely bouquet of flowers in his shirt frill. He was beautifully frizzed and powdered, and had a magnificent queue hanging down his back. The little sword at his side seemed to be made entirely of jewels, it sparkled and shone so, and the little hat under his arm was woven of flocks of silk. He gave proof of the fineness of his manners in that he had brought for Marie a quantity of the most delightful toys—above all,

the very same figures as those which the mouse king had eaten up—as well as a beautiful sabre for Fritz. He cracked nuts at table for the whole party; the very hardest did not withstand him. He placed them in his mouth with his left hand, tugged at his pigtail with his right, and crack! they fell in pieces.

Marie grew red as a rose at the sight of this charming young gentleman; and she grew redder still when, after dinner, young Drosselmeier asked her to go with him to the glass cupboard in the sitting-room.

"Play nicely together, children," said Godpapa Drosselmeier; "now that my clocks are all nicely in order, I can have no possible objection."

But as soon as young Drosselmeier was alone with Marie, he went down on one knee, and spake as follows:

"Ah! my most dearly-beloved Miss Stahlbaum! see here at your feet the fortunate Drosselmeier, whose life you saved here on this very spot. You were kind enough to say, plainly and unmistakably, in so many words, that you would not have despised me, as Princess Pirlipat did, if I had been turned ugly for your sake. Immediately I ceased to be a contemptible Nutcracker, and resumed my former not altogether ill-looking person and form. Ah! most exquisite lady! bless me with your precious hand; share with me my crown and kingdom, and reign with me in Marchpane Castle, for there I now am king."

Marie raised him, and said gently:

"Dear Mr. Drosselmeier, you are a kind, nice gentleman; and as you reign over a delightful country of charming, funny, pretty people, I accept your hand."

So then they were formally betrothed; and when a year and a day had come and gone, they say he came and fetched her away in a golden coach, drawn by silver horses. At the marriage there danced two-and-twenty thousand of the most beautiful dolls and other figures, all glittering in pearls and diamonds; and Marie is to this day the queen of a realm where all kinds of sparkling Christmas Woods, and transparent Marchpane Castles—in short, the most wonderful and beautiful things of every kind—are to be seen—by those who have the eyes to see them.

So this is the end of the tale of the Nutcracker and the Mouse King.

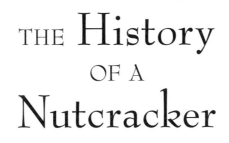

THE History
OF A
Nutcracker

Alexandre Dumas

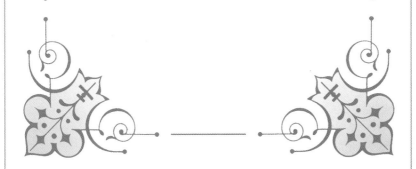

Preface

Which Shows How the Author was Forced to Relate the History of the Nutcracker of Nuremberg

There was a juvenile party at the house of my friend Lord M—; and I had helped to add to the number and noise of the company by taking my little daughter.

It is true that in half an hour, during which I joined in four or five games of blind-man's buff, hot cockles, and hunt the slipper—in spite of the noise which was made by a couple of dozen delightful little rogues from eight to ten years old, and who seemed to try which would talk the loudest—I slipt out of the drawing-room, and sought a certain snug parlour which I knew, and where I hoped to enjoy a little peace for an hour or so.

I had effected my retreat with as much skill as success, escaping not only without being perceived by the juvenile guests, which was not very difficult, considering how intent they were upon their games, but also unnoticed by their parents, which was not so easy a matter. I had reached the wished-for parlour, when I observed, on entering it, that it was for the moment converted into a supper-room, the side boards being heaped up with confectionary and other refreshments. Now as these appearances seemed to promise that I should not be disturbed until supper-time, I threw myself into a comfortable arm-chair, quite delighted with the idea that I was about to enjoy an hour's peace after the dreadful noise which had deafened me in the drawing-room.

I don't know exactly how it was, but at the end of about ten minutes I fell fast asleep.

I cannot say how long I had thus lost all knowledge of what was passing around, when I was suddenly aroused by loud peals of laughter. I opened my eyes in terror, and saw nothing but the beautifully-painted ceiling over my head. Then I tried to get up; but the attempt was useless, for I was fastened to my chair as firmly as Gulliver was on the shore of Lilliput.

I immediately understood in what a scrape I had got myself: I had been surprised in the enemy's country, and was a prisoner of war.

The best thing for me to do in such a case was to put a good face upon the matter, and entreat for my liberty.

My first proposal was to take my conquerors the very next morning to Farrance's, and treat them to anything they liked; but, unhappily, the moment was not well chosen for such an offer: I was addressing myself to an audience already well stuffed with tarts, and whose hands were filled with patties.

My proposal was therefore refused in plain terms.

I then offered to take the entire party to Vauxhall next evening, and amuse them with the exhibition of fire-works.

The proposal was well-received by the little boys; but the little girls would not listen to it, because they were dreadfully afraid of fire-works: they could not endure the noise of the crackers, and the smell of the gunpowder annoyed them.

I was about to make a third offer, when I heard a sweet little musical voice whispering in the ears of a companion certain words which made me tremble: "Ask papa, who writes novels, to tell us some pretty story."

I was on the point of protesting against this; but my voice was drowned by cries of "Oh! yes, a story—we will have a story!"

"But, my dear children," I said, as loud as I could, "you ask me the most difficult thing in the world. A story indeed! Ask me to recite one of Gay's fables, or *My Name is Norval*, if you will; and I may consent. But a story!"

"We don't want anything out of the *Speaker*," cried the children altogether: "we want a story!"

"My dear little friends, if—"

"There is no *if* in the cause: we will have a story!"

"But, my dear little friends, I say again—"

"There is no *but*: we will have a story!"

"Yes: we will have a story! we will have a story!" now echoed on all sides, and in a manner which was too positive to object to any longer.

"Well," I said with a sign: "if you must, you must."

"Ah! that's capital," cried my little tormentors.

"But I must tell you one thing," said I: "the story I am about to relate is not my own."

"Never mind that, so long as it amuses us."

I must confess that I was a little vexed to think that my audience set so light a value upon my own writings.

"Whose tale is it, then, sir!" asked a pretty voice, belonging, no doubt, to some little being more curious than the others.

"It is by Hoffmann, miss. Have you ever heard of Hoffmann?"

"No, sir; I never heard of him."

"And what is the name of your story, sir?" asked a young gentleman, who, being the son of the nobleman that gave the party, felt a right to question me.

"*The History of a Nutcracker*," was my answer. Does the title please you, my dear Henry?"

"Hem! I don't think the title promises anything particularly fine. But, never mind; go on! If it does not please us, we will stop you, and you must begin another; and so on, I can tell you, until you really do fix upon a good one."

"One moment!" I exclaimed. "I will not accept those conditions. If you were grown-up persons, well and good!"

"Nevertheless, those are our conditions: if not, a prisoner you must remain with us for ever."

The Nutcracker.

"My dear Henry, you are a charming boy—well brought up—and I shall be much surprised if you do not some day become Prime Minister of England. Let me go free, and I will do all you ask."

"On your word of honour?"

"On my word of honour."

At the same moment I felt the thousand threads that held me suddenly become loose: each of the little tormentors had set to work to untie a knot; and in half a minute I was at liberty.

Now as every one must keep his word, even when it is pledged to children, I desired my audience to sit round me; and when the children had all placed themselves in a manner so comfortable that I fancied they would soon fall off to sleep in their chairs, I began my story in the following manner.

GODFATHER DROSSELMAYER

Once upon a time there lived at Nuremberg, in Germany, a judge of great respectability, and who was called Judge Silberhaus, which means "silver-house."

This judge had a son and daughter. The son was nine years old, and was named Fritz: the daughter, who was seven and a half, was called Mary.

They were two beautiful children; but so different in disposition and features, that no one would have believed them to be brother and sister.

Fritz was a fine stout boy with ruddy cheeks and roguish looks. He was very impatient, and stamped on the floor whenever he was contradicted; for he thought that everything in the world had been made for his amusement, or to suit his fancy. In this humour he would remain until the judge, annoyed by his cries and screams, or by his stamping, came out of his study, and, raising his fore-finger, said with a frown, "Master Fritz!"

These two words were quite sufficient to make Master Fritz wish that the earth would open and swallow him up.

As for his mother, it was no matter how much or how often she raised her fore-finger; for Fritz did not mind her at all.

His sister Mary was, on the contrary, a delicate and pale child, with long hair curling naturally, and flowing over her little white shoulders like a flood of golden light upon a vase of alabaster. She was sweet, amiable, bashful, and kind to all who were in sorrow, even to her dolls: she was very obedient to her mamma, and never contradicted her governess, Miss Trudchen; so that Mary was beloved by every one.

Now, the 24th of December, 17. . ., had arrived. You all know, my dear young friends, that the 24th of December is called Christmas Eve, being the day before the one on which the Redeemer Jesus was born.

But I must now explain something to you. You have all heard, perhaps, that every country has its peculiar customs; and the best read amongst you are aware that Nuremberg, in Germany, is a town famous for its toys, puppets, and playthings, of which it exports great quantities to other countries. You will admit, therefore, that the little boys and girls of Nuremberg ought to be the happiest children in the world, unless, indeed, they are like the inhabitants of Ostend, who seem only to delight in their oysters for the purpose of sending them to foreign markets. Germany, being quite a different country from England, has altogether other customs. In England, New Year's Day is the grand day for making

presents, so that many parents would be very glad if the year always commenced with the 2nd of January.

But in Germany the great day for presents is the 24th of December, the one preceding Christmas Day. Moreover, in Germany, children's presents are given in a peculiar way. A large shrub is placed upon a table in the drawing-room; and to all its branches are hung the toys to be distributed among the children. Such play-things as are too heavy to hang to the shrub, are placed on the table; and the children are then told that it is their guardian angel who sends them all those pretty toys. This is a very innocent deception, after all; and perhaps it can scarcely be called a deception, because all the good things of this world are sent to us by heaven.

I need scarcely tell you that among those children of Nuremberg who received most presents were the son and daughter of Judge Silberhaus; for besides their father and mother, who doted on them, they also had a godfather who loved them dearly, and whose name was Drosselmayer.

I must describe in a few words the portrait of this illustrious person, who occupied in the town of Nuremberg a position almost as high as that of Judge Silberhaus himself.

Godfather Drosselmayer, who was a great physician and doctor of medicine, was by no means a very good-looking person. He was a tall thin man, about six feet high, but who stooped very much, so that, in spite of the length of his legs, he could almost pick up his handkerchief, if it fell, without stooping any lower. His face was wrinkled as a golden rennet that has withered and fallen from the tree. Being blind of the right eye, he wore a black patch; and, being entirely bald, he wore a shining and frizzled wig, which he had made himself with spun glass, such as you may have seen the glass-blowers spin at the Adelaide Gallery or Polytechnic Institution. He was, however, compelled, for fear of damaging this ingenious contrivance, to carry his hat under his arm.

His remaining eye was sparkling and bright, and seemed not only to perform its own duty, but that of its absent companion, so rapidly did it glance round any room which Godfather Drosselmayer was desirous to scrutinize in all points, or fix upon any person whose secret thoughts he wished to read.

Now, Godfather Drosselmayer, who was a learned doctor, did not follow the example of those physicians who allow their patients to die, but occupied his time in giving life to dead things: I mean that, by studying the formation of men and animals, he had gained so deep a knowledge of the manner in which they are made, that he was able to manufacture men who could walk, bow to each other, and go through their exercises with a musket. He also made ladies who danced, and played upon the harpsichord, the harp, and the viol; dogs that ran, carried, and barked; birds that flew, hopped, and sang; and fish that swam, and ate crumbs of bread. He had even succeeded in making puppets and images of Punch utter a few words—not many, it is true, but such as "papa," "mamma," &c. The tones were certainly harsh, and always the same in sound; because you can very well understand that all this was done merely by means of machinery concealed inside the toys; and no machinery can ever perform the same wonders as the beings which God has created.

Nevertheless, in spite of all difficulties, Godfather Drosselmayer did not despair of being some day able to make real men, real women, real dogs, real birds, and real fish. It is scarcely necessary to add that his two god-children, to whom he had promised the first proofs of his success in this line, awaited the happy moment with great impatience.

Godfather Drosselmayer, having reached this state of perfection in mechanical science, was a most useful man to his friends. Thus, for instance, if a time-piece at the house of Judge Silberhaus got out of

order, in spite of the attentions of the usual clock-makers—if the hands
suddenly stopped—if the tick-tick seemed to go badly—or if the wheels
inside would not move—Godfather Drosselmayer was immediately
sent for; and he hastened to the house as quick as he could, for he was a
man devoted to the art of mechanics. He was no sooner shown the poor
clock, than he instantly opened it, took out the works, and placed them
between his knees. Then, with his eye glittering like a carbuncle, and his
wig laid upon the floor, he drew from his pocket a number of little tools
which he had made himself, and the proper use of which he alone knew.
Choosing the most pointed one, he plunged it into the very midst of the
works, to the great alarm of little Mary, who could not believe that the
poor clock did not suffer from the operation. But in a short time when
the old gentleman had touched the works in various parts, and placed
them again in their case, or on their stand, or between the four pillars of
the time-piece, as the case might be, the clock soon began to revive, to
tick as loud as ever, and to strike with its shrill clear voice at the proper

time; a circumstance that gave new life, as it were, to the room itself, which without it seemed a melancholy place.

Moreover, in compliance with the wishes of little Mary, who was grieved to see the kitchen dog turning the spit, Godfather Drosselmayer made a wooden dog, which by means of mechanism connected inside, turned the spit without annoyance to itself. *Turk*, who had done this duty for three years, until he had become quite shaky all over, was now able to lie down in peace in front of the kitchen fire, and amuse himself by watching the movements of his successor.

Thus, after the judge, after the judge's wife, after Fritz, and after Mary, the dog Turk was certainly the next inmate of the house who had most reason to love and respect Godfather Drosselmayer. Turk was indeed grateful, and showed his joy, whenever Drosselmayer drew near the house, by leaping up against the front door and wagging his tail, even before the old gentleman had knocked.

On the evening of the 24th of December, just as the twilight was approaching, Fritz and Mary, who had not been allowed to enter the drawing-room all day, were huddled together in a corner of the dining-parlour. Miss Trudchen, the governess, was knitting near the window, to which she had moved her chair, in order to catch the last rays of day-light. The children were seized with a kind of vague fear, because candles had not been brought into the room, according to custom; so they were talking in a low tone to each other, just as children talk when they are afraid.

"Fritz," said Mary, "I am sure papa and mamma are busy in preparing the Christmas tree; for ever since the morning I have heard a great deal going on in the drawing-room, which we were forbidden to enter."

"And I know," said Fritz, "by the way Turk barked ten minutes ago, that Godfather Drosselmayer has arrived."

"Oh! I wonder what our dear kind godfather has brought us!" exclaimed Mary, clapping her little hands. "I am sure it will be a beautiful garden, planted with trees, and with a beautiful river running between the banks, covered with flowers. And on the river, too, there will be some silver swans with collars of gold, and a little girl will bring them sweet-cake, which they will eat out of her apron."

"In the first place, Miss," said Fritz, in that authoritative tone which was natural to him, and which his parents considered to be one of his greatest faults, "you must know that swans do not eat sweet-cake."

"I thought they did," answered Mary; "but as you are a year and a half older than I, you must know best."

Fritz tossed his head up with an air of importance.

"And, for my part," he continued, "I feel certain that if Godfather Drosselmayer brings anything at all, it will be a castle with soldiers to watch it, and enemies to attack it. We shall then have some famous battles."

"I do not like battles," said Mary. "If he does bring a castle, as you think he will, it must be for you: I shall, however, take care of the wounded."

"Whatever it is that he brings," returned Fritz, "you know very well that it is neither for you nor for me; because the toys which Godfather Drosselmayer gives us are always taken away again immediately afterwards, under pretence that they really are works of great art. Then, you know, they are always put into that great cupboard with the glass doors, and on the top shelves, which papa himself can only reach when he stands upon a chair. So, after all, I much prefer the toys which papa and mamma give us, and which we are allowed to play with until we break them into a thousand pieces."

"And so do I," answered Mary; "only we must not say so to godfather."

"And why not?"

"Because he would feel annoyed to think that we do not like his toys as much as those which papa and mamma give us. He gives them to us, thinking to please us; and it would be wrong to tell him the contrary."

"Oh! nonsense," cried Fritz.

"Miss Mary is quite right, Master Fritz," said Dame Trudchen, who was generally very silent, and only spoke on important occasions.

"Come," said Mary hastily, in order to prevent Fritz from giving an impudent answer to the poor governess; "let us guess what our parents intend to give us. For my part I told mamma—but upon condition that she would not scold—that Miss Rose, my doll, grows more and more awkward, in spite of the lessons which I am constantly giving her; and that she does nothing but fall upon her nose, which never fails to leave most disagreeable marks upon her face; so that I can no longer take her into decent society, because her face does not at all correspond with her frocks."

"And I," said Fritz, "did not hesitate to assure papa that a nice little horse would look admirably well in my stables; I also took the opportunity to inform him that no army can possibly exist without cavalry, and that I want a squadron of hussars to complete the division which I command."

These words made Miss Trudchen conclude that the moment was favourable for her to speak a second time.

"Master Fritz and Miss Mary," said she, "you know very well that it is your guardian angel who sends and blesses all those fine toys which are given to you. Do not therefore say beforehand what you want; because the angel knows much better than you what will please you."

"Oh!" cried Fritz; "and yet last year he sent me foot soldiers, although, as I have just said, I should have been better satisfied with a squadron of hussars."

"For my part I have only to thank my good angel," said Mary; "for did I but ask for a doll last year, and I not only had the doll, but also a beautiful white dove with red feet and beak."

In the meantime the night had altogether drawn in, and the children, who by degrees spoke lower and lower, and grew closer and closer together, fancied that they heard the wings of their guardian angels fluttering near them, and a sweet music in the distance, like that of an organ accompanying the Hymn of the Nativity, beneath the gloomy arches of a cathedral. Presently a sudden light shone upon the wall for a moment, and Fritz and Mary believed that it was their guardian angel, who, after depositing in the toys in the drawing-room, flew away in the midst of a golden lustre to visit other children who were expecting him with the same impatience as themselves.

Immediately afterward a bell rang—the door was thrown violently open—and so strong a light burst into the apartment that the children were dazzled, and uttered cries of surprise and alarm.

The judge and his wife then appeared at the door, and took the hands of their children, saying, "Come, little dears, and see what the guardian angels have sent you."

The children hastened to the drawing-room; and Miss Trudchen, having placed her work upon a chair, followed them.

THE CHRISTMAS TREE

My dear children, you all know the beautiful toy-stalls in the Soho Bazaar, the Pantheon, and the Lowther Arcade; and your parents have often taken you there, to permit you to choose whatever you liked best. Then you have stopped short, with longing eyes and open mouth; and you have experienced a pleasure which you will never again know in your lives—no, not even when you become men and acquire titles or fortunes. Well, the same joy was felt by Fritz and Mary when they entered the drawing-room and saw the great tree growing as it were from the middle of the table, and covered with blossoms made of sugar, and sugar-plums instead of fruit—the whole glittering by the light of a hundred Christmas candles concealed amidst the leaves. At the beautiful sight Fritz leapt for joy, and danced about in a manner which showed how well he had attended to the lessons of his dancing-master. On her side, Mary could not restrain two large tears of joy which, like liquid pearls, rolled down her countenance, that was open and smiling as a rose in June. But the children's joy knew no bounds when they came to examine all the pretty things which covered the table. There was a beautiful doll, twice as large as Miss Rose; and there was also a charming silk frock, hung on a stand in such a manner that Mary could walk around it. Fritz was also well pleased; for he found upon the table a squadron of hussars, with red jackets and gold lace, and mounted on white horses; while on the carpet, near the table, stood the famous horse which he also much longed to see in his stables. In a moment did this modern Alexander leap upon the back of that brilliant Bucephalus, which was already saddled and bridled; and, having ridden two or three times around the table, he got off again, declaring that though the animal was very spirited and restive, he should soon be able to tame him in such a manner that ere a month passed the horse would be quiet as a lamb.

But at the moment when Fritz set his foot upon the ground, and when Mary was baptising her new doll by the name of Clara, the bell rang a second time; and the children turned towards that corner of the room when the sound came.

They then beheld something which had hitherto escaped their attention, so intent had they been upon the beautiful Christmas tree. In fact, the corner of the room of which I have just spoken, was concealed, or cut off as it were, by a large Chinese screen, behind which there was a certain noise accompanied by a certain sweet music, which proved that something unusual was going on in that quarter. The children then recollected that they had not yet seen the doctor; and they both exclaimed at the same moment, "Oh! Godpapa Drosselmeyer!"

At these words—and as if it had only waited for that exclamation to put itself in motion—the screen opened inwards, and showed not only Godfather Drosselmayer, but something more!

In the midst of a green meadow, decorated with flowers, stood a magnificent country-seat, with numerous windows, all made of real glass, in front, and two gilt towers on the wings. At the same moment the jingling of bells was heard from within—the doors and windows opened—and the rooms inside were discovered lighted up by wax-tapers half an inch high. In those rooms were several little gentlemen and ladies, all walking about: the gentlemen splendidly dressed in laced coats, and silk waistcoats and breeches, each with a sword by his side, and a hat under his arm; the ladies gorgeously attired in brocades, their hair dressed in the style of the eighteenth century, and each one holding a fan in her hand, wherewith they all fanned themselves as if overcome by the heat. In the central drawing-room, which actually seemed to be on fire, so splendid was the lustre of the crystal chandelier, filled with wax candles, a number of children were dancing to the jingling music; the boys all in round jackets, and the girls all in short frocks. At the same time a gentleman, clad in a furred cloak, appeared at the window of an adjoining chamber, made signs, and then disappeared again; while Godfather Drosselmayer himself, with his drab frock-coat, the patch on his eye, and the glass wig—so like the original, although only three inches high, that the puppet might be taken for the doctor, as if seen at a great distance—went out and in the front door of the mansion with the air of a gentleman, inviting those who were walking outside to enter his abode.

The first moment was one of surprise and delight for the two children; but, having watched the building for a few minutes with his elbows resting on the table, Fritz rose and exclaimed, "But, Godpapa Drosselmayer, why do you keep going out and coming in by the same door? You must be tired of going backwards and forwards like that. Come, enter by that door there, and come out by this one here."

And Fritz pointed with his finger to the doors of the two towers.

"No, that cannot be done," answered Godfather Drosselmayer.

"Well, then," said Fritz, "do me the pleasure of going up those stairs, and taking the place of that gentleman at the window: then tell him to go down to the door."

"It is impossible, my dear Fritz," again said the doctor.

"At all events the children have danced enough: let them go and walk, while the gentlemen and ladies who are now walking, dance in their turn."

"But you are not reasonable, you little rogue," cried the godpapa, who began to grow angry: "the mechanism must move in a certain way."

"Then let me go into the house," said Fritz.

"Now you are silly, my dear boy," observed the judge: "you see that it is impossible for you to enter the house, since the vanes on the top of the towers scarcely come up to your shoulders."

Fritz yielded to this reasoning and held his tongue; but in a few moments, seeing that the ladies and gentlemen kept on walking, that the children would not leave off dancing, that the gentleman with the furred cloak appeared and disappeared at regular intervals, and that Godfather Drosselmayer did not leave the door, he again broke his silence.

"My dear godpapa," said he, "if all these little figures can do nothing more than what they are doing over and over again, you may take them away to-morrow, for I do not care about them; and I like my horse much better, because it runs when I choose— and my hussars, because they manœuvre at my command, and wheel to the right or left, or march forward or backward, and are not shut up in any house like your poor little people who can only move over and over in the same way.

With these words he turned his back upon Godfather Drosselmayer and the house, hastened to the table, and drew up his hussars in battle array.

As for Mary, she had slipped away very gently, because the motions of the little figures in the house seemed to her to be very tiresome: but as she was a charming child, she said nothing, for fear of wounding the feelings of Godpapa Drosselmayer. Indeed, the moment Fritz turned his back, the doctor said to the judge and his wife, in a tone of vexation, "This masterpiece is not fit for children; and I will put my house back again into the box, and take it away."

But the judge's wife approach him, and, in order to atone for her son's rudeness, begged Godfather Drosselmayer to explain to her all the secrets of the beautiful house, and praised the ingenuity of the mechanism to such an extent, that she not only made the doctor forget his vexation, but put him into such a good humour, that he drew from the pockets of his drab coat a number of little men and women with horn complexions, white eyes, and gilt hands and feet. Besides the beauty of their

appearance, these little men and women set forth a delicious perfume, because they were made of cinnamon.

At this moment Miss Trudchen called Mary, and offered to help her to put on the pretty little silk frock which she had so much admired on first entering the drawing-room; but Mary, in spite of her usual politeness, did not answer the governess, so much was she occupied with a new personage whom she had discovered amongst the toys, and to whom, my dear children, I must briefly direct your attention, since he is actually the hero of my tale, in which Miss Trudchen, Mary, Fritz, the judge, the judge's lady, and even Godfather Drosselmayer, are only secondary characters.

The Little Man with the Wooden Cloak

I told you that Mary did not reply to the invitation of Miss Trudchen, because she had just discovered a new toy which she had not before perceived.

Indeed, by dint of making his hussars march and counter-march about the table, Fritz had brought to light a charming little gentleman, who, leaning in a melancholy mood against the trunk of the Christmas tree, awaited, in silence and polite reserve, the moment when his turn to be inspected should arrive. We must pause to notice the appearance of this little man, to whom I gave the epithet "charming" somewhat hastily; for, in addition to his body being too long and large for the miserable little thin legs which supported it, his head was of a size so enormous that it was quite at variance with the proportions indicated not only by nature, but also by those drawing-masters who know much better than even Nature herself.

But if there were any fault in his person, that defect was atoned for by the excellence of his toilette, which denoted at once a man of education and taste. He wore a braided frock coat of violet-coloured velvet, all frogged and covered with buttons; trousers of the same material; and the most charming little Wellington boots ever seen on the feet of a student or an officer. But these were two circumstances which seemed strange in respect to a man who preserved such elegant taste: the one was an ugly narrow cloak made of wood, and which hung down like a pig's tale from the nape of his neck to the middle of his back; and the other was a wretched cap, such as peasants sometimes wear in Switzerland, upon his head. But Mary, when she perceived those two objects which seemed so unsuitable to the rest of the costume, remembered that Godfather Drosselmayer himself wore above his drab coat a little collar of no better appearance than the wooden cloak belonging to the little gentleman in the military frock; and that the doctor often covered his own bald head with an ugly—an absolutely frightful cap, unlike all other ugly caps in the world—although this circumstance did not prevent the doctor from being an excellent godpapa. She even thought to herself that were Godpapa Drosselmayer to imitate altogether the dress of the little gentleman with the wooden cloak, he could not possibly become so genteel and interesting as the puppet.

You can very well believe that these reflections on the part of Mary were not made without a close inspection of the little man, whom she liked from the very first moment that she saw him. Then, the more she looked at him, the more she was struck by the sweetness and amiability which were expressed by his countenance. His clear green eyes, which were certainly rather goggle, beamed with serenity and kindness. The frizzled beard of white cotton, extending beneath his chin, seemed to become him amazingly, because it set off the charming smile of his mouth, which was rather wide perhaps; but then, the lips were as red as vermilion!

Thus was it that, after examining the little man for upwards of ten minutes, without daring to touch it, Mary exclaimed, "Oh! dear papa, whose is that funny figure leaning against the Christmas tree?"

"It belongs to no one in particular," answered the judge; "but to both of you together."

"How do you mean, dear papa? I do not understand you."

"This little man," continued the judge, "will help you both; for it is he who in future will crack all your nuts for you; and he belongs as much to Fritz as to you, and as much to you as Fritz."

Thus speaking, the judge took up the little man very carefully, and raising his wood cloak, made him open his mouth by a very simple motion, and display two rows of sharp white teeth. Mary then placed a nut in the little man's mouth; and crack—crack—the shell was broken into a dozen pieces, and the kernel fell whole and sound into Mary's hand. The little girl then learnt that the dandified gentleman belonged to that ancient and respectable race of Nutcrackers whose origin is as ancient as that of the town of Nuremberg, and that he continued to exercise the honourable calling of his forefathers. Mary, delighted to have made this discovery, leapt for joy; whereupon the Judge said, "Well, my dear little Mary, since the Nutcracker pleases you so much, although it belongs equally to Fritz and yourself, it is to you that I especially trust it. I place it in your care."

With these words the judge handed the little fellow to Mary, who took the puppet in her arms, and began to practise it in its vocation, choosing, however—so good was her heart—the smallest nuts, that it might not be compelled to open its mouth to wide, because by so doing its face assumed a most ridiculous expression. Then Miss Trudchen drew near to behold the little puppet in her turn; and for her also did it perform its duty in the most unassuming and obliging manner in the world, although she was but a dependant.

While he was employed in training his horse and parading his Hussars, Master Fritz heard the crack—crack so often repeated, that he felt sure something new was going on. He accordingly looked up and turned his large inquiring eyes upon the group composed of the judge, Mary, and Miss Trudchen; and when he observed the little man with the wooden cloak in his sister's arms, he leapt from his horse, and, without waiting to put the animal in its stable, hastened towards Mary. Then what a joyous shout of laughter burst from his lips as he espied the funny appearance of the little man opening his large mouth. Fritz also demanded his share of the nuts which the puppet cracked; and this was of course granted. Next he wanted to hold the little man while he cracked the nuts; and this wish was also gratified. Only, in spite of the remonstrances of his sister, Fritz chose the largest and hardest nuts to cram into his mouth; so that at the fifth of sixth c-r-r-ack! and out fell three of the poor little fellow's teeth. At the same time his chin fell and became tremulous like that of an old man.

"Oh! my poor Nutcracker!" ejaculated Mary, snatching the little man from the hands of Fritz.

"What a stupid fellow he is!" cried the boy: "he pretends to be a Nutcracker, and his jaws are as brittle as glass. He is a false Nutcracker, and he does not understand his duty. Give him to me, Mary; I will make him go on cracking my nuts, even if he loses all his teeth in doing so, and his chin is dislocated entirely. But how you seem to feel for the lazy fellow!"

"No—no—no!" cried Mary, clasping the little man in her arms:

"no—you shall not have my Nutcracker! See how he looks at me, as much as to tell me that his poor jaw is hurt. Fie, Fritz! you are very ill-natured—you beat your horses; and the other day you shot one of your soldiers."

"I beat my horses when they are restive," said Fritz, with an air of importance; "and as for the soldier whom I shot the other day, he was a wretched scoundrel that I never have been able to do anything with for the last year, and who deserted one fine morning with his arms and baggage—a crime that is punishable by death in all countries. Besides, all these things are matters of discipline which do not regard women. I do not prevent you from boxing your doll's ears; so don't try to hinder me from whipping my horses or shooting my soldiers. But I want the Nutcracker."

"Papa—papa!—help—help!" cried Mary, wrapping the little man in her pocket-handkerchief: "help! Fritz is going to take the Nutcracker from me!"

At Mary's cries, not only the judge drew near the children; but his wife and Godfather Drosselmayer also ran towards them. The two children told their stories in their own way—

Mary wishing to keep the Nutcracker, and Fritz anxious to have it again. But to the astonishment of Mary, Godfather Drosselmayer, with a smile that seemed perfectly frightful to the poor little girl, decided in favor of Fritz. Happily for the poor Nutcracker, the judge and his wife took little Mary's part.

"My dear Fritz," said the judge, "I trusted the Nutcracker to the care of your sister; and as far as my knowledge of surgery goes, I see that the poor creature is unwell and requires attention. I therefore give him over solely to the care of Mary, until he is quite well; and no one must say a word against my decision. And you, Fritz, who stand up so firmly in behalf of military discipline, when did you ever hear of making a wounded soldier return to his duty? The wounded always go to the hospital until they are cured; and if they be disabled by their wounds, they are entitled to pensions."

Fritz was about to reply; but the judge raised his forefinger to a level with his right eye, and said, "Master Fritz!"

You have already seen what influence those two words had upon the little boy: thus, ashamed at having drawn upon himself the reprimand

conveyed in those words, he slipped quietly off, without giving any answer, to the table where his hussars were posted: then, having placed the sentinels in their stations, he marched off the rest to their quarters for the night.

In the meantime Mary picked up the three little teeth which had fallen from the Nutcracker's mouth, and kept the Nutcracker himself well wrapped up in the pocket-handkerchief; she had also bound up his chin with a pretty white ribbon which she cut from the frock. On his side, the little man, who was at first very pale and much frightened, seemed quite contented in the care of his protectress, and gradually acquired confidence, when he felt himself gently rocked in her arms. Then Mary perceived that Godfather Drosselmayer watched with mocking smiles the care which she bestowed upon the little man with the wooden cloak; and it struck her that the single eye of the doctor had acquired an expression of spite and malignity which she had never before seen. She therefore tried to get away from him; but Godfather Drosselmayer burst out laughing, saying, "Well, my dear goddaughter, I am really astonished that a pretty girl like you can be so devoted to an ugly little urchin like that."

Mary turned round; and much as she loved her godfather, even the compliment which he paid her did not make amends for the unjust attack he made upon the person of her Nutcracker. She even felt—contrary to her usual disposition—very angry; and that vague comparison which she had before formed between the little man with the wooden cloak and her godfather, returned to her memory.

"Godpapa Drosselmayer," she said, "you are unkind towards my little Nutcracker, whom you call an ugly urchin. Who knows whether you would even look so well as he, even if you had his pretty little military coat, his pretty little breeches, and his pretty little boots!"

At these words Mary's parents burst out laughing; and the doctor's nose grew prodigiously longer.

Why did the doctor's nose grow so much longer? Mary, surprised by the effect of her remark, could not guess the reason.

But there are never any effects without causes, that reason no doubt belonged to some strange and unknown cause, which we must explain.

Wonderful Events

I do not know, my dear little friends, whether you remember that I spoke of a certain large cupboard, with glass windows, in which the children's toys were locked up. This cupboard was on the right side of the door of the judge's own room. Mary was still a baby in the cradle, and Fritz had only just began to walk, when the judge had that cupboard made by a very skilful carpenter, who put such brilliant glass in the frames, that the toys appeared a thousand times finer when ranged on the shelves than when they were held in the hand. Upon the top shelf of all, which neither Fritz nor Mary could reach, the beautiful pieces of workmanship of Godfather Drosselmayer were placed. Immediately beneath was the shelf containing the picture-books; and the two lower shelves were given to Fritz and Mary, who filled them in the way they liked best. It seemed, however, to have been tacitly agreed upon between the two children, that Fritz should hold possession of the higher shelf of the two, for the marshalling of his troops, and that Mary should keep the lower shelf for her dolls and their households. This arrangement

was entered into on the eve of Christmas Day. Fritz placed his soldiers upon his own shelf; and Mary, having thrust Miss Rose into a corner, gave the bed-room, formed by the lowest shelf, to Miss Clara, with whom she invited herself to pass the evening and enjoy a supper of sugar plums. Miss Clara, on casting her eyes around, saw that everything was in proper order; her table well spread with sugar plums and conserved fruits, and her nice white bed with its white counterpane, all so neat and comfortable. She therefore felt very well satisfied with her new apartment.

While all these arrangements were being made, the evening wore away: midnight was approaching—Godfather Drosselmayer had been gone a long time—and yet the children could not be persuaded to quit the cupboard.

Contrary to custom, it was Fritz that yielded first to the persuasion of his parents, who told him that it was time to go to bed.

"Well," said he, "after all the exercise which my poor hussars have had to-day, they must be fatigued; and as those excellent soldiers all know their duty towards me—and as, so long as I remain here, they will not close their eyes—I must retire."

With these words—and having given them the watch-word, to prevent them from being surprised by a patrol of the enemy—Fritz went off to bed.

But this was not the case with Mary; and as her mamma, who was about to follow her husband to their bed-chamber, desired her to tear herself away from the dearly-beloved cupboard, little Mary said, "Only one moment, dear mamma—a single moment: do let me finish all I have to do here. There are a hundred or more important things to put to rights; and the moment I have settled them, I promise to go to bed."

Mary requested this favour in so touching and plaintive a tone—she was, moreover, so glad and obedient a child—that her mother did not hesitate to grant her request. Nevertheless, as Miss Trudchen had already gone up stairs to get Mary's bed ready, the judge's wife, thinking that her daughter might forget to put out the candles, performed that duty herself, leaving only a light in the lamp hanging from the ceiling.

"Do not be long before you go to your room, dear little Mary," said the judge's wife; "for if you remain up too long, you will not be able to rise at your usual hour to-morrow morning."

With these words the lady quitted the room and closed the door behind her.

The moment Mary found herself alone, she bethought herself, above all things, of her poor little Nutcracker; for she contrived to keep it in her arms, wrapped up in her pocket handkerchief. She placed him upon the table very gently, unrolled her handkerchief, and examined his chin. The Nutcracker still seemed to suffer much pain, and appeared very cross.

"Ah! my dear little fellow," she said in a low tone, "do not be angry, I pray, because my brother Fritz hurt you so much. He had no evil intention, rest well assured; only his manners have become rough, and his heart is a little hardened by his soldier's life. Otherwise he is a very good boy, I can assure you; and I know that when you are better acquainted with him, you will forgive him. Besides, to atone for the injury which he has done you, I will take care of you; which I will do so attentively that in a few days you will be quite well. As for putting in the teeth again and fastening your chin properly, that is the business of Godpapa Drosselmayer, who perfectly understands those kinds of things."

Mary could say no more; for the moment she pronounced the name of her Godfather Drosselmayer, the Nutcracker, to whom this discourse was addressed, made so dreadful a grimace, and his eyes suddenly flashed so brightly, that the little girl stopped short in affright, and stepped a pace back. But as the Nutcracker immediately afterwards resumed its amiable expression and its melancholy smile, she fancied that she must have been the sport of an illusion, and that the flame of the lamp, agitated by a current of air, had thus disfigured the little man. She even laughed at herself, saying, "I am indeed very foolish to think that this wooden puppet could make faces to me. Come, let me draw near the poor fellow, and take that care of him which he requires."

Having thus mused within herself, Mary took the puppet once more in her arms, drew near the cupboard, knocked at the glass door, which Fritz had closed, and said to the new doll, "I beg of you, Miss Clara, to give up your bed to my poor Nutcracker, who is unwell, and to shift for yourself on the sofa to-night. Remember that you are in excellent health yourself, as your round and rosy cheeks sufficiently prove. Moreover, a night is soon passed; the sofa is very comfortable, and there will not be many dolls in Nuremberg as well lodged as yourself."

Miss Clara, as you may well suppose, did not utter a word; but it struck Mary that she seemed very sulky and discontented; but Mary, whose conscience told her that she had treated Miss Clara in the most considerate manner, used no farther ceremony with her, but, drawing the bed towards her, placed the Nutcracker in it, covering him with the clothes up to the very chin: she then thought that she knew nothing as yet of the real disposition of Miss Clara, whom she had only seen for a few hours; but that as Miss Clara had appeared to be in a very bad humour at losing her bed, some evil might happen to the poor invalid if he were left with so insolent a person. She therefore placed the bed, with the Nutcracker in it, upon the second shelf, close by the ridge where Fritz's cavalry were quartered: then, having laid Miss Clara upon the sofa, she closed the cupboard, and was about to rejoin Miss Trudchen in the bed-chamber, when all around the room the poor girl heard a variety of low scratching sounds coming from behind the chairs, the store, and the cupboard. The large clock which hung against the wall, and which was surmounted by a large gilt owl, instead of a cuckoo, as is usual with old German clocks, began that usual whirring sound which gives warning of striking; and yet it did not strike. Mary glanced towards it, and saw that the immense gilt owl had drooped its wings in such a way that they covered the entire clock, and that the bird thrust forward as far as it could its hideous cat-like head, with the round eyes and the crooked beak. Then the whirring sound of the clock became louder and louder, and gradually changed into the resemblance of a human voice, until it appeared as if these words issued from the beak of the owl: "Clocks, clocks, clocks! whir, whir, whir! in a low tone! The king of the mice has a sharp ear! Sing him his old song! Strike, strike,

strike, clocks all: sound his last hour—for his fate is night at hand!"

And then, dong—dong—dong—the clock struck twelve in a hollow and gloomy tone.

Mary was very much frightened. She began to shudder from head to foot; and she was about to run away from the room, when she beheld Godfather Drosselmayer seated upon the clock instead of the owl, the two skirts of his coat having taken the place of the drooping wings of the bird. At that spectacle, Mary remained nailed as it were to the spot with astonishment; and she began to cry, saying, "What are you doing up there, Godpapa Drosselmayer? Come down here, and don't frighten me like that, naughty Godpapa Drosselmayer."

But at these words there began a sharp whistling and furious kind of tittering all around: then in a few moments Mary heard thousands of little feet treading behind the walls; and next she saw thousands of little lights through the joints in the wainscot. When I say little lights, I am wrong—I mean thousands of little eyes. Mary full well perceived that there was an entire population of mice about to enter the room. And, in fact, in the course of five minutes, thousands and thousands of mice made their appearance by the creases of the door and the joints of the floor, and began to gallop hither and thither, until at length they ranged themselves in order of

battle, as Fritz was wont to draw upon his wood soldiers. All this seemed very amusing to Mary; and as she did not feel towards mice that absurd alarm which so many foolish children experience, she thought she should divert herself with the sight, when there suddenly rang through the room a whistling so sharp, so terrible, and so long, that a cold shudder passed over her.

At the same time, a plank was raised up by some power underneath, and the king of the mice, with seven heads all wearing gold crowns, appeared at her very feet, in the midst of the mortar and plaster that was broken up; and each of his seven mouths began to whistle and scream horribly, while the body to which those seven heads belonged forced its way through the opening. The entire army advanced towards the king, speaking with their little mouths three times in chorus. Then the various regiments marched across the room, directing their course towards the cupboard, and surrounding Mary on all sides, so that she began to beat a retreat. I have already told you that Mary was not a timid child; but when she saw herself surrounded by crowds of mice, commanded by that monster with seven heads, fear seized upon her, and her heart began to beat so violently, that it seemed as if it would burst from her chest. Her blood appeared to freeze in her veins, her breath failed her; and, half fainting, she retreated with trembling steps. At length—pir-r-r! and the pieces of the panes in the cupboard, broken by her elbow which knocked against it, fell upon the floor. She felt at the moment an acute pain in the left arm; but at the same time her heart grew lighter, for she no longer heard that squeaking which had so much frightened her. Indeed, everything had again become quiet around her; the mice had disappeared; and she thought that, terrified by the noises of the glass which was broken, they had sought refuge in their holes.

But almost immediately afterwards a strange noise commenced in the cupboard; and numerous little sharp voices exclaimed, "To arms! to arms! to arms!" At the same time the music of Godfather Drosselmayer's country-house, which had been placed upon the top shelf of the cupboard, began to play; and on all sides she heard the words, "Quick! rise to arms! to arms!"

Mary turned round. The cupboard was lighted up in a wondrous manner, and all was bustle within. All the harlequins, the clowns, the punches, and the other puppets scampered about; while the dolls set to work to make lint and prepare bandages for the wounded. At length the Nutcracker himself threw off all the clothes, and jumped off the bed, crying, "Foolish troop of mice! return to your holes, or you must encounter me!"

But at that menace a loud whistling echoed through the room; and Mary perceived that the mice had not returned to their holes; but that, frightened by the noise of the broken glass, they had sought refuge beneath the chairs and tables, whence they were now beginning to issue again.

On his side, Nutcracker, far from being terrified by the whistling, seemed to gather fresh courage.

"Despicable king of the mice," he exclaimed; "it is thou, then! Thou acceptest the death which I have so long offered you? Come on, and let this night decide between us. And you, my good friends—my companions—my brethren, if it be indeed true that we are united in bonds of affection, support me in this perilous contest! On! on!—let those who love me follow!"

Never did a proclamation produce such an effect. Two harlequins, a clown, two punches, and three other puppets, cried out in a loud tone, "Yes, my lord, we are your's in life and death! We will conquer under your command, or die with you!"

At these words, which proved that there was an echo to his speech in the heart of his friends, Nutcracker felt himself so excited, that he drew his sword, and without calculating the dreadful height on which he stood, leapt from the second shelf. Mary, upon perceiving that dangerous leap, gave a piercing cry; for Nutcracker seemed on the point of being dashed to pieces; when Miss Clara, who was on the lower shelf, darted from the sofa and received him in her arms.

"Ah! my dear little Clara," said Mary, clasping her hands together with emotion: "how have I mistaken your disposition!"

But Miss Clara, thinking only of the present events, said to the Nutcracker, "What! my lord—wounded and suffering as you are, you are plunging headlong into new dangers! Content yourself with

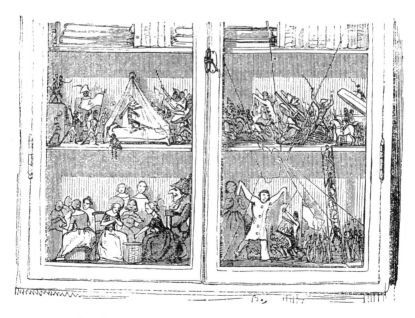

commanding the army, and let the others fight. Your
courage is known; and you can do no good by giving
fresh proof of it!"

And as she spoke, Clara endeavoured to restrain
the gallant Nutcracker by holding him tight in her
arms; but he began to struggle and kick in such
a manner that Miss Clara was obliged to let him
glide down. He slipped from her arms, and fell on
his knees at her feet in a most graceful manner,
saying, "Princess, believe me, that although at a
certain period you were unjust towards me, I shall
always remember you, even in the midst of battle!"

Miss Clara stooped as low down as possible, and, taking him by
his little arm, compelled him to rise: then taking off her waist-band all
glittering with spangles, she made a scarf of it, and sought to pass it over
the shoulder of the young hero; but he, stepping back a few paces, and
bowing at the same time in acknowledgment of so great a favour, untied
the little white ribbon with which Mary had
bound up his chin, and tied it round his waist,
after pressing it to his lips. Then, light as a bird,
he leapt from the shelf on the floor, brandishing
his sabre all the time. Immediately did the
squeakings and creakings of the mice begin over
again; and the king of the mice, as if to reply
to the challenge of the Nutcracker, issued from
beneath the great table in the middle of the
room, followed by the main body of his army.
At the same time, the wings, on the right and
left, began to appear from beneath the arm-
chair, under which they had taken refuge.

The Battle

"Trumpets, sound the charge! drums, beat the alarm!" exclaimed the valiant Nutcracker.

And at the same moment the trumpets of Fritz's hussars began to sound, while the drums of his infantry began to beat, and the rumbling of canon was also heard. At the same time a band of musicians was formed with fat Figaros with their guitars, Swiss peasants with their horns, and Negroes with their triangles. And all these persons, though not called upon by the Nutcracker, did not the less begin to descend from shelf to shelf, playing the beautiful march of the "British Grenadiers." The music no doubt excited the most peaceably-inclined puppets; for, at the same moment, a kind of militia, commanded by the beadle of the parish, was formed, consisting of harlequins, punches, clowns, and pantaloons. Arming themselves with anything that fell in their way, they were soon ready for battle. All was bustle, even to a man-cook, who, quitting his fire, came down with his spit, on which was a half-roasted turkey, and went and took his place in the ranks. The Nutcracker placed himself at the head of this valiant battalion, which, to the shame of the regular troops, was ready first.

I must tell you everything, or else you might think that I am inclined to be too favourable to that glorious militia; and therefore I must say that if the infantry and cavalry of Master Fritz were not ready so soon as the others, it was because they were all shut up in four boxes. The poor prisoners might therefore well hear the trumpet and drum which called them to battle: they were shut up, and could not get out. Mary heard them stirring in their boxes, like cray-fish in a basket; but, in spite of their efforts, they could not free themselves. At length the grenadiers, less tightly fastened in than the others, succeeded in raising the lid of their box, and then helped to liberate the light infantry. In another instant, these were free; and, well knowing how useful cavalry is in a battle, they hastened to release the hussars, who began to canter gaily about, and range themselves four deep upon the flanks.

But if the regular troops were thus somewhat behindhand, in consequence of the excellent discipline in which Fritz maintained them, they speedily repaired the lost time: for infantry, cavalry, and artillery began to descend with the fury of an avalanche, amidst the plaudits of Miss Rose and Miss Clara, who clapped their hands as they passed, and encouraged them with their voices, as the ladies from whom they were descended most likely were wont to do in the days of ancient chivalry.

Meantime the king of the mice perceived that he had to encounter an entire army. In fact, the Nutcracker was in the centre of his gallant band of militia; on the left was the regiment of hussars, waiting only the moment to charge; on the right was stationed a formidable battalion of infantry; while, upon a footstool which commanded the entire scene of battle, was a park of ten cannon. In addition to these forces, a powerful reserve, composed of gingerbread men, and warriors made of sugar of different colours, had remained in the cupboard, and already began to bustle about. The king of the mice had, however, gone too far to retreat; and he gave the signal by a squeak, which was repeated by all the forces under his command.

At the same moment the battery on the footstool replied with a volley of shot amongst the masses of mice.

The regiment of hussars rushed onward to the charge, so that on one side the dust raised by their horses feet, and on the other the smoke of the cannon, concealed their plain of battle from the eyes of Mary.

But in the midst of the roar of cannon, the shouts of the combatants, and the groans of the dying, she heard the voice of the Nutcracker ever rising above the din.

"Serjeant Harlequin," he cried, "take twenty men, and fall upon the flank of the enemy. Lieutenant Punch, form into a square. Captain Puppet, fire in platoons. Colonel of Hussars, charge in masses, and not four deep, as you are doing. Bravo, good leaden soldiers—bravo! If all my troops behave as well as you, the day is ours!"

But, by these encouraging words even, Mary was at no loss to perceive that the battle was deadly,

and that the victory remained doubtful. The mice, thrown back by the hussars—decimated by the fire of platoons—and shattered by the park of artillery, returned again and again to the charge, biting and tearing all who came in their way. It was like the combats in the days of chivalry—a furious struggle foot to foot and hand to hand, each one bent upon attack or defence, without waiting to think of his neighbour. Nutcracker vainly endeavoured to direct the evolutions in a disciplined manner, and form his troops into dense columns. The hussars, assailed by numerous corps of mice, were scattered, and failed to rally round their colonel; a vast battalion of enemy had cut them off from the main body of their army, and had actually advanced up to the militia, which performed prodigies of valour. The beadle of the parish used his battle-axe most gallantly; the man-cook ran whole ranks of mice through with his spit; the leaden soldiers remained firm as a wall; but Harlequin and his twenty men had been driven back, and were forced to retreat under cover of the battery; and Lieutenant Punch's square had been broken up. The remains of his troops fled and threw the militia into disorder; and Captain Puppet, doubtless for want of cartridges, had ceased to fire, and was in full retreat. In consequence of this backward movement through the line, the park of cannon was exposed. The king of the mice, perceiving that the success of the fight depend upon the capture of that battery, ordered his bravest troops to attack it. The footstool was accordingly stormed in a moment, and the artillerymen were cut to pieces by the side of their cannon. One of them set fire to his powder-waggon, and met an heroic death with twenty of his comrades. But all this display was useless against numbers; and in a short time a volley of shot, fired upon them from their own cannon, and which swept the forces commanded by the Nutcracker, convinced him that the battery of the footstool had fallen into the hands of the enemy.

From that moment the battle was lost, and the Nutcracker now thought only of beating an honourable retreat: but, in order to give breathing time to his troops, he summoned the reserve to his aid.

Thereupon, the gingerbread men and the corps of sugar warriors descended from the cupboard and took part in the battle. They were certainly fresh, but very inexperienced, troops: the gingerbread men especially were very awkward, and, hitting right and left, did as much injury to friends as to enemies. The sugar warriors stood firm; but they were of such different natures—emperors, knights, Tyrolese peasants, gardeners, cupids, monkeys, lions, and crocodiles—that they could not combine their movements, and were strong only as a mass. Their arrival, however, produced some good; for scarcely had the mice tasted

the gingerbread men and the sugar warriors, when they left the leaden soldiers, whom they found very hard to bite, and turned also from the punches, harlequins, beadles, and cooks, who were only stuffed with brann, to fall upon the unfortunate reserve, which in a moment was surrounded by thousands of mice, and, after an heroic defense, devoured arms and baggage.

Nutcracker attempted to profit by that moment to rally his army; but the terrible spectacle of the destruction of the reserve had struck terror to the bravest hearts. Captain puppet was as pale as death; Harlequin's clothes were in rags; a mouse had penetrated into Punch's hump, and, like the youthful Spartan's fox, began to devour his entrails; and not only was the colonel of the hussars a prisoner with a large portion of his troops, but the mice had even formed a squadron of cavalry, by means of horses thus taken.

The unfortunate Nutcracker had no chance of victory left: he could not even retreat with honour; and therefore he determined to die.

He placed himself at the head of a small body of men, resolved like himself to sell their lives dearly.

In the meantime terror reign:d among the dolls: Miss Clara and Miss Rose wrung their hands, and gave vent to loud cries.

"Alas!" exclaimed Miss Clara; "must I die in the flower of my youth—I, the daughter of a king, and born to such brilliant destinies?"

"Alas!" said Miss Rose; "am I doomed to fall into the hands of the enemy, and be devoured by the filthy mice?"

The other dolls ran about in tears; their cries mingling with those of Miss Clara and Miss Rose. Meanwhile matters went worse and worse with Nutcracker: he was abandoned by the few friends who had remained faithful to him. The remains of the squadron of hussars took refuge in the cupboard; the leaden soldiers had all fallen into the power of the enemy; the cannoneers had long previously been dispersed; and the militia was cut to pieces, like the three hundred Spartans of Leonidas, without yielding a step. Nutcracker had planted himself against the lower part of the cupboard, which he vainly sought to climb up: he could not do so without the aid of Miss Rose or Miss Clara; and they had found nothing better to do than to faint. Nutcracker made a last effort, collected all his courage, and cried in an agony of despair, "A horse! a horse! my kingdom for a horse!" But, as in the case of Richard III, his voice remained without even an echo—or rather betrayed him to the enemy. Two of the rifle-brigade of the mice seized upon his wooden cloak; and at the same time the king of the mice cried with his seven mouths, "On your heads, take him alive! Remember that I have my mother to avenge! This punishment must serve as an example to all future Nutcrackers!"

And, with these words, the king rushed upon the prisoner.

But Mary could no longer support that horrible spectacle.

"Oh! my poor Nutcracker!" she exclaimed: "I love you with all my heart, and cannot see you die thus!"

At the same moment, by a natural impulse and without precisely knowing what she was doing, Mary took off one of her shoes, and threw it with all her force in the midst of the combatants. Her aim was

so good that the shoe hit the king of the mice, and made him roll over in the dust. A moment afterwards, king and army—conquerors and conquered—all alike disappeared, as if by enchantment. Mary felt a more severe pain than before in her arm. She endeavoured to reach an arm-chair to sit down; but her strength failed her—and she fainted!

THE ILLNESS

When Mary awoke from her deep sleep, she found herself lying in her little bed, and the sun penetrated radiant and brilliant through the windows. By her side was seated a gentleman whom she shortly perceived to be a surgeon named Vandelstern, and who said in a low voice, the moment she opened her eyes, "She is awake."

Then the judge's wife advanced towards the bed, and gazed upon her daughter for a long time with an anxious air.

"Ah! my dear mamma," exclaimed little Mary, upon seeing her mother; "are all those horrible mice gone? and is my poor Nutcracker saved?"

"For the love of heaven, my dear Mary, do not repeat all that nonsense," said the lady. "What have mice, I should like to know, to do with the Nutcracker? But you, naughty girl, have frightened us all sadly. And it is always so when children are obstinate and will not obey their parents. You played with your toys very late last night: you most likely fell asleep; and it is probable that a little mouse frightened you. At all events, in your alarm, you thrust your elbow

through one of the panes of the cupboard, and cut your arm in such a manner that Mr. Vandlestern, who has just extracted the fragments of glass, declares that you ran a risk of cutting an artery and dying through loss of blood. Heaven be thanked that I awoke—I know not at what o'clock—and that, recollecting how I had left you in the room, I went down to look after you. Poor child! you were stretched upon the floor, near the cupboard; and all round you were strewed the dolls, the puppets, the punches, the leaden soldiers, pieces of the gingerbread men, and Fritz's hussars—all scattered about pell-mell—while in your arms you held the Nutcracker. But how was it that you had taken off one of your shoes, and that it was at some distance from you?"

"Ah! my dear mother," said Mary, shuddering as she thought of what had taken place; "all that you saw was caused by the great battle that took place between the puppets and the mice: but the reason of my terror was that I saw the victorious mice about to seize upon the poor Nutcracker, who commanded the puppets;—and it was then that I threw my shoe at the king of the mice. After that, I know not what happened."

The surgeon made a sign to the judge's lady, who said in a soft tone to Mary, "Do not think any more of all that, my dear child. All the mice are gone, and the little Nutcracker is safe and comfortable in the glass cupboard."

The judge then entered the room, and conversed for a long time with the surgeon; but of all that they said Mary could only catch these words—"It is delirium."

Mary saw immediately that her story was not believed, but that it was looked upon as fable; and

she did not say any more upon the subject, but allowed those around her to have their own way. For she was anxious to get up as soon as possible and pay a visit to the poor Nutcracker. She, however, knew she had escaped safe and sound from the battle; and that was all she cared about for the present.

Nevertheless Mary was very restless. She could not play, on account of her wounded arm; and when she tried to read or look over her picture-books, everything swam so before her eyes that she was obliged to give up the task. The time hung very heavily upon her hands; and she looked forward with impatience to the evening, because her momma would come and sit by her, and tell her pleasant stories.

One evening, the judge's wife had just ended the pretty tale of "Prince Facardin," when the door opened, and Godfather Drosselmayer thrust in his head, saying, "I must see with my own eyes how the little invalid gets on."

But when Mary perceived Godfather Drosselmayer with his glass wig, his black patch, and his drab frock coat, the remembrance of the night when the Nutcracker lost the famous battle against the mice, returned so forcibly to her mind, that she could not prevent herself from crying out, "O Godpapa Drosselmayer, you were really very ugly! I saw you quite plainly, when you were astride upon the clock, and when you covered it with your wings to prevent it from striking, because it would have frightened away the mice. I heard you call the king with the seven heads. Why did you not come to the aid of my poor Nutcracker, naughty Godpapa Drosselmayer; for, by not coming, you were the cause of my hurting myself and having to keep to my bed."

The judge's wife listened to all this with a kind of stupor; for she thought that the poor little girl was relapsing into delirium. She therefore said, in a low tone of alarm, "What are you talking about, Mary? are you taking leave of your senses?"

"Oh! no," answered Mary; "and Godpapa Drosselmayer knows that I am telling the truth."

But the godfather, without saying a word, made horrible faces, like a man who was sitting upon thorns; then all of a sudden he began to chaunt these lines in a gloomy sing-song tone:—

> "Old Clock-bell, beat
>> Low, dull, and hoarse:—
> Advance, retreat,
>> Thou gallant force!
>
> The bell's lone sound proclaims around
>> The hour of deep mid-night;
> And the piercing note from the screech-owl's throat
>> Puts the king himself to flight.
>
> Old clock-bell, beat
>> Low, dull, and hoarse:—
> Advance, retreat,
>> Thou gallant force!"

Mary contemplated Godfather Drosselmayer with increasing terror; for he now seemed to her more hideously ugly than usual. She would indeed have been dreadfully afraid of him, if her mother had not been present, and if Fritz had not at that moment entered the room with a loud shout of laughter.

"Do you know, Godpapa Drosselmayer," said Fritz, "that you are uncommonly amusing to-day: you seem to move about just like my punch that stands behind the store; and, as for the song, it is not common sense."

"My dear doctor," she said, "your song is indeed very strange, and appears to me to be only calculated to make little Mary worse."

"Nonsense!" cried Godfather Drosselmayer: "do you not recognise the old chant which I am in the habit of humming when I mend your clocks?"

At the same time he seated himself near Mary's bed, and said to her in a rapid tone, "Do not be angry with me, my dear child, because I did not tear out the fourteen eyes of the king of the mice with my own hands; but I knew what I was about—and now, as I am anxious to make it up with you, I will tell you a story."

"What story?" asked Mary.

"*The History of the Crackatook Nut and Princess Pirlipata*. Do you know it?"

"No, my dear godpapa," replied Mary, whom the offer of a story reconciled to the doctor that moment. "Go on."

"My dear doctor," said the judge's wife, "I hope that your story will not be so melancholy as your song?"

"Oh, no, my dear lady," returned Godfather Drosselmayer. "On the contrary, it is very amusing."

"Tell it to us, then!" cried both the children.

Godfather Drosselmayer accordingly began in the following manner.

* * * * *

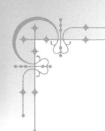

The History of the Crackatook Nut
and Princess Pirlipata

How Princess Pirlipata Was Born, and How the Event
Produced the Greatest Joy to Her Parents

There was lately, in the neighbourhood of Nuremberg, a little kingdom, which was not Prussia, nor Poland, nor Bavaria, nor the Palatinate, and which was governed by a king.

This king's wife, who was consequently a queen, became the mother of a little girl, who was therefore a princess by birth, and received the sweet name of Pirlipata.

The king was instantly informed of the event, and he hastened out of breath to see the pretty infant in her cradle. The joy which he felt in being the father of so charming a child, carried him to such an extreme that, quite forgetting himself, he uttered loud cries of joy, and began to dance around the room, crying, "Oh! who has ever seen anything so beautiful as my Pirlapatetta?"

Then, as the king had been followed into the room by his ministers, his generals, the great officers of state, the chief judges, the councilors, and the puisne judges, they all began dancing around the room as the king, singing:

"Great monarch, we ne'er
In this world did see
A child so fair
As the one that there
Has been given to thee!
Oh! ne'er, and Oh! ne'er,
Was there child so fair!"

And, indeed—although I may surprise you by saying so—there was not a word of flattery in all this; for, since the creation of the world, a sweeter child than Princess Pirlipata never has been seen. Her little face appeared to be made of the softest silken tissue, like the white rosy tints of the lily combined. Here eyes were of the purest and brightest blue; and nothing was more charming than to behold the golden thread of her hair, flowing in delicate curls over shoulders as white as alabaster. Moreover, Pirlipata, when born, was already provided with two complete rows of the most pearly teeth, with which—two hours after her birth—she bit the finger of the lord chancellor so hard, when, being near sighted, he stooped down to look close at her, that, although he belonged to the sect of stoic philosophers, he cried out according to some, "Oh! the dickens!" whereas others affirm, to the honour of philosophy, that he only said, "Oh! Oh!" However, up to the present day opinions are divided upon this important subject, neither party being willing to yield to the other. Indeed, the only point on which the *Dickensonians* and the *Ohists* are agreed is, that the princess really did bite the finger of the lord high chancellor. The country thereby learnt that there was as much spirit as beauty belonging to the charming Pirlipata.

Everyone was therefore happy in a kingdom so blest by heaven, save the queen herself, who was anxious and uneasy, no person knew why. But what chiefly struck people with surprise, was the care with which the timid mother had the cradle of the infant watched. In fact, besides having all the doors guarded by sentinels, and in addition to the two regular nurses, the queen had six other nurses to sit round the cradle, and who were relieved by a half-a-dozen others at night. But what caused the greatest interest, and which no one could understand, was that each of these six nurses was compelled to hold a cat upon her knees, and to tickle it all night so as to prevent it from sleeping, and keep it purring.

I am certain, my dear children, that you are as curious as the inhabitants of that little kingdom without a name, to know why these extra nurses were forced to hold cats upon their knees, and to tickle them in such a way that they should never cease purring; but, as you would vainly endeavour to find out the secret of that enigma,

DIOLOT

I shall explain it to you, in order to save you the headache which would not fail to be the result of your guess-work.

It happened one day that half-a-dozen great kings took it into their heads to pay a visit to the future father of Princess Pirlipata, for at that time the princess was not born. They were accompanied by the royal princes, the hereditary grand dukes, and the heirs apparent, all most agreeable personages. This arrival was the signal for the king whom they visited, and who was a most hospitable monarch, to make a large drain upon his treasury, and give tournaments, feasts, and dramatic representations. But this was not all. He having learnt from the intendant of the royal kitchen, that the astronomer royal of the court was favourable for killing pigs, and the conjunction of the stars foretold that the year would be propitious for sausage-making, the king commanded a tremendous slaughter of pigs to take place in the court-yard. Then, ordering his carriage, he went in person to call upon all the kings and princes staying in his capital, and invite them to dine with him; for he was resolved to surprise them by the splendid banquet which he intended to give them. On his return to the palace, he retired to the queen's apartment, and going to her, said

in a coaxing tone, with which he was always accustomed to make her do anything he wished, "My most particular and very dear love, you have not forgotten—have you—how doatingly fond I am of black puddings? You surely have not forgotten that?"

The queen understood by the first word what the king wanted of her. In fact she knew by his cunning address, that she must now proceed, as she had done many times before, to the very useful occupation of making, with her own royal hands, the greatest possible quantity of sausages, polonies, and black puddings. She therefore smiled at that proposal of her husband; for although filling with dignity the high situation of queen, she was less proud of the compliments paid her upon the manner in which she bore the sceptre and the crown, than of those bestowed on her skill in making a black pudding, or any other dish. She therefore contented herself by curtseying gracefully to her husband, saying that she was quite ready to make him the puddings which he required.

The grand treasurer accordingly received orders to carry the immense enamelled cauldron and the large silver saucepans to the royal kitchens, so that the queen might make the black puddings, the polonies, and the sausages. An enormous fire was made with sandal-wood; the queen put on her apron of white damask, and in a short time delicious odours steamed from the cauldron. Those sweet perfumes spread through the passages, penetrated into all the rooms, and reached the throne room where the king was holding a privy council. The king was very fond of good eating, and

the smell made a profound impression upon him. Nevertheless, as he was a wise prince, and was famed for his habits of self-command, he resisted for a long time the feeling which attracted him towards the kitchens; but at last, in spite of the command which he exercised over himself, he was compelled to yield to the inclination that now ruled him.

"My lords and gentlemen," he accordingly said, rising from his throne, "with your permission I will retire for a few moments; pray wait for me." Then this great king hastened through the passages and corridors to the kitchen, embraced his wife tenderly, stirred the contents of the cauldron with his golden sceptre, and tasted them with the tip of his tongue. Having thus calmed his mind, he returned to the council, and resumed, though somewhat abstractedly, the subject of discussion.

He had left the kitchen just at the important moment when the fat, cut up in small pieces, was about to be broiled upon the silver gridirons. The queen, encouraged by his praises, now commenced that important operation; and the first drops of grease had just dripped upon the live coals, when a squeaking voice was heard to chant the following lines:

"Dear sister, pray give to the queen of the Mice,
A piece of that fat which is grilling so nice;
To me a good dinner is something so rare,
That I hope of the fat you will give me a share."

The queen immediately recognised the voice that thus spoke; it was the voice of Dame Mousey.

Dame Mousey had lived for many years in the palace. She declared herself to be a relation of the royal family, and was Queen of the kingdom of Mice. She therefore maintained a numerous court beneath the kitchen hearth-stone.

The queen was a kind and good-natured woman; and although she would not publicly recognise Dame Mousey as a sister and a sovereign, she nevertheless showed her in private a thousand flattering attentions. Her husband, more particular than herself, had often reproached her for thus lowering herself. But on the present occasion she could not find it in her heart to refuse the request of her little friend; and she accordingly said, "Come, Dame Mousey, without fear, and taste my pork-fat as much as you like. I give you full leave to do so."

Dame Mousey accordingly leapt upon the hearth, quite gay and happy, and took with her little paws the pieces of fat which the queen gave her.

But, behold! the murmurs of joy which escaped the mouth of Dame Mousey, and the delicious smell of the morsels of fat on the gridiron, reached her seven sons, then her relations, and next her friends, all of whom were terribly addicted to gourmandizing, and who now fell upon the fat with such fury, that the queen was obliged, hospitable as she was, to remind them that if they continued at that rate only five minutes more, there would not be enough fat left for the black puddings. But, in spite of the justice of this remonstrance, the seven sons of Dame Mousey took no heed of them; and setting a bad example to their relations and friends, rushed upon their aunt's fat, which would have entirely disappeared, had not the cries of the queen brought the man-cook and scullery boys, all armed with brushes and brooms, to drive the mice back again under the hearth-stone. But the victory, although complete, came somewhat too late; for there scarcely remained a quarter enough fat necessary for the polonies, the sausages, and the black puddings. The remnant, however, was scientifically divided by the royal mathematician, who was sent for in all possible haste, between the large cauldron containing the materials for the puddings, and the two saucepans in which the sausages and polonies were cooking.

Half an hour after this event, the cannon fired, the clarions and trumpets sounded, and then came the potentates, the royal princes, the hereditary dukes, and the heirs apparent to the thrones, all dressed in their most splendid clothes, and some riding on gallant chargers. The king received them on the threshold of the palace, in the most courteous manner possible; then, having conducted them to the banqueting room, he took his seat at the head of the table in his quality of sovereignhood, and having the crown upon his head and the sceptre in his hand. The guests all placed themselves at table according to their rank, as crowned kings, royal princes, hereditary dukes, or heirs apparent.

The board was covered with dainties, and everything went well during the soup and the first course. But when the polonies were placed on the table, the king seemed to be agitated; when the sausages were served up, he grew very pale; and when the black puddings were brought in, he raised his eyes to heaven, sighs escaped his breast, and a terrible grief seemed to rend his soul. At length he fell back in his chair, and covered his face with his hands, sobbing and moaning in so lamentable a manner, that all the guests rose from their seats and surrounded him with great anxiety. At length the crisis seemed very serious; the court physician could not feel the beating of the pulse of the unfortunate monarch, who was thus overwhelmed with the weight of the most profound, the most frightful, and the most unheard of calamity. At length, upon the most violent remedies, such as burnt feathers, volatile salts, and cold keys thrust down the back, had been employed, the king seemed to return to himself. He opened his eyes, and said in a scarcely audible tone, "*not enough fat!*"

At these words, the queen grew pale in her turn, she threw herself at his feet, crying in a voice interrupted by sobs, "Oh! my unfortunate, unhappy, and royal husband, What grief have I not caused you, by refusing to listen to the advice which you have so

often given me! But you behold the guilty one at your feet, and you can punish her as severely as you think fit."

"What is the matter?" demanded the king, "and what has happened that I know not of?"

"Alas! alas!" answered the queen, to whom her husband had never spoken in so cross a tone; "Alas! Dame Mousey, her seven sons, her nephews, her cousins, and her friends, devoured the fat."

But the queen could not say any more; her strength failed her, she fell back and fainted.

Then the king rose in a great rage, and cried in a terrible voice, "Let her ladyship the royal housekeeper explain what all this means! Come, speak!"

Then the royal housekeeper related all that she knew; namely, that being alarmed by the queen's cries, she ran and beheld the majesty beset by the entire family of Dame Mousey, and that, having summoned the cooks and scullery boys, the plunderers were compelled to retreat.

The king, perceiving that this was a case of high treason, resumed all his dignity and calmness, and commanded the privy council to meet that minute, the matter being of the utmost importance. The council assembled, the business was explained, and it was decided by a majority of voices, "That Dame Mousey, being accused of having eaten the fat destined for the sausages,

the polonies, and the black puddings of the king, should be tried for the same offence; and that if the said Dame Mousey was found guilty, she and all her race should be banished from the kingdom, and all her good or possessions, namely, lands, castles, palaces, and royal residencies should be confiscated."

Then the king observed to his councillors that while the trial lasted, Dame Mousey and her family would have sufficient time to devour all the fat in the royal kitchens, which would expose him to the same privation as that which he had just endured in the presence of six crowned heads, without reckoning royal princes, hereditary dukes, and heirs apparent. He therefore demanded a discretionary power in respect to dame Mousey and her family.

The privy council divided, for the form of the thing, but the discretionary power was voted, as you may well suppose, by a large majority.

Then the king sent one of his best carriages, preceded by a courier that greater speed might be used, to a very skilful mechanic who lived at Nuremberg, and whose name was Christian Elias Drosselmayer.

This mechanic was requested to proceed that moment to the palace upon urgent business. Christian Elias Drosselmayer immediately obeyed, for he felt convinced that the king required him to make some work of art. Stepping into the vehicle, he travelled day and night, until he arrived in the king's presence. Indeed, such was his haste, that he had not waited to change the drab-coloured coat which he usually wore. But instead of being angry at that breach of etiquette, the king was much pleased with his haste; for if the famous mechanic had committed a fault, it was in his anxiety to obey the kings commands.

The king took Christian Elias Drosselmayer into his private chamber, and explained to him the position of affairs; namely, that it was decided upon to make a striking example of the race of mice throughout the kingdom; that attracted by the fame of his skill, the king had fixed upon him to put the decree of justice into execution; and that the said king's only fear was lest the mechanic, skilful though he were, should perceive insurmountable difficulties in the way of appeasing the royal anger.

But Christian Elias Drosselmayer reassured the king, promising that in eight days there should not be a single mouse left in the kingdom.

In a word, that very same day he set to work to make several ingenious little oblong boxes, inside which he placed a morsel of fat at the end of a piece of wire. By seizing upon the fat, the plunderer, whoever he might be, caused the door to shut down behind him, and thus became a prisoner. In less than a week, a hundred of these boxes were made, and placed, not only beneath the hearthstone, but in all the garrets, lofts, and cellars of the palace. Dame Mousey was far too cunning and sagacious not to discover at the first glance the stratagem of Master

Drosselmayer. She therefore assembled her seven sons, their nephews, and their cousins, to warn them of the snare that was laid for them. But, after having appeared to listen to her, and the veneration which her years commanded, they withdrew, laughing at her terrors; then, attracted by the smell of the fried pork-fat, they resolved, in spite of the representations made to them, to profit by the charity that came they knew not whence.

At the expiration of twenty-four hours, the seven sons of Dame Mousey, eighteen of her nephews, fifty of her cousins, and two hundred and thirty-five of her other connexions, without reckoning thousands of her subjects, were caught in the mouse-traps and ignominiously executed.

Then did Dame Mousey, with the remnant of her court and the rest of her subjects, resolve upon abandoning a place covered with the blood of her massacred relatives and friends. The tidings of that resolution became known and reached the ears of the king. His majesty expressed his satisfaction, and the poets of the court composed sonnets upon his victory, while the courtiers compared him to Sesostris, Alexander, and Cæsar.

The queen was alone anxious and uneasy; she knew Dame Mousey well, and suspected that she would not leave unavenged the death of her relations and friends. And, in fact, at the very moment when the

queen, by way of atoning for her previous fault, was preparing with
her own hands a liver soup for the king, who doated upon that dish,
Dame Mousey suddenly appeared and chanted the following lines:

Thine husband, void of pity and of fear,
Hath slain my cousins, sons, and nephews dear;
    But list, O Queen! to the decrees of fate:
The child which heaven will shortly give to thee,
And which the object of thy love will be,
    Shall bear the rage of my vindictive hate.

Thine husband owneth castles, cannons, towers,
A council's wisdom, and an army's powers,
    Mechanics, ministers, mouse-traps, and snares:
None of all these, alas! to me belong;
But heaven hath given me teeth, sharp, firm, and strong,
    That I may rend in pieces royal heirs.

Having sung these words she disappeared, and no one saw her
afterwards. But the queen, who expected a little baby, was so overcome
by the prophecy, that she upset the liver soup into the fire.

Thus, for the second time, was Dame Mousey the
cause of depriving the king of one of his favourite
dishes, whereat he fell into a dreadful rage. He,
however, rejoiced more than ever at the step he had
taken to ride his country of the mice.

It is scarcely necessary to say that Christian
Edward Drosselmayer was sent away well rewarded,
and returned in triumph to Nuremberg.

* * * * *

How, in Spite of the Precautions Taken
by the Queen, Dame Mousey Accomplishes
Her Threat in Regard to Princess Pirlipata

And now, my dear children, you know as well as I do, wherefore
the queen had Princess Pirlipata watched with such wonderful care.
She feared the vengeance of Dame Mousey; for, according to what
Dame Mousey had said, there could be nothing less in store for the
heiress of this little kingdom without a name, than the loss of her
life, or at all events her beauty; which last affliction is considered by
some people worse for one of her sex. What redoubled the fears of
the queen was, that the machines invented by Master Drosselmayer
were totally useless against the experience of Dame Mousey. The
astronomer of the court, who was also grand prophet and grand
astrologer, was fearful lest his office should be suppressed unless he
gave his opinion at this important juncture: he accordingly declared
that he read in the stars the great fact that the illustrious family of
the cat Murr was alone capable of defending the cradle against the
approach of Dame Mousey. It was for this reason that each of his
six nurses was forced to hold a cat constantly upon her knees. Those
cats might be considered as under-officers attached to the court;

and the nurses sought to lighten the
cares of the duty performed by
the cats, by gently rubbing
them with their fair
hands.

You know, my dear
children, that there are
certain times when a
person watches even
while actually dozing;

and so it was that, one evening, in spite of all the efforts which the six nurses made to the contrary, as they sate round the cradle of the princess with the cats upon their knees, they felt sleep rapidly gaining upon them. Now, as each nurse kept her own ideas to herself, and was afraid of revealing them to their companions, hoping all the time that their drowsiness would not be perceived by others, the result was, that, one after another, they closed their eyes—their hands stopped from stroking the cats—and the cats themselves, being no longer rubbed and scratched, profited by circumstance to take a nap.

I cannot say how long this strange slumber had lasted, when, towards midnight, one of the nurses awoke with a start. All the others were in a state of profound lethargy: not a sound—not even their very breathing, was heard: the silence of death reigned around, broken only by the slight creak of the worm biting the wood. But how frightened was the nurse when she beheld a large and horrible mouse standing up near her on its hind legs, and, having plunged its head into the cradle, seemed very busy in biting the face of the princess! She rose with a cry of alarm; and at that exclamation, all the other nurses jumped up. But Dame Mousey—for she indeed it was—sprang towards one corner of the room. The cats leapt after her: alas! it was too late—Dame Mousey had disappeared by a crevice in the floor. At the same moment Princess Pirlipata, who was awoke by all that din, began to cry. Those sounds made the nurses leap with joy. "Thank God!" they said; "since Princess Pirlipata cries she is not dead!" They then all ran towards the cradle—but their despair was great indeed when they saw what had happened to that delicate and charming creature!

In fact, instead of that face of softly blended white and red—that little head, with its golden hair—those mild blue eyes, azure as the sky itself—instead of all these charms the nurses beheld an enormous and mis-shapen head upon a deformed and ugly body. Her two sweet eyes had lost their heavenly hue, and became goggle, fixed, and haggard. Her little mouth had grown from ear to ear; and her chin was covered with a beard like grizzly cotton. All this would have suited old Punch; but seemed very horrible for a young princess.

At that moment the queen entered. The twelve nurses threw themselves with their faces against the ground; while the six cats walked about to discover if there were not some open window by which they might escape upon the tiles. At the sight of her child the despair of the poor mother was something frightful to behold; and she was carried off in a fainting fit into the royal chamber. But it was chiefly the unhappy father whose sorrow was the most desperate and painful to witness. The courtiers were compelled to put padlocks upon the windows, for fear he should throw himself out; and they were also forced to line the walls with mattresses, lest he should dash out his brains against them. His sword was of course taken away from him; and neither knife nor fork, nor any sharp or pointed instruments were left in his way. This was the more easily effected; inasmuch as he ate nothing for the two or three following days, crying without ceasing, "Oh! miserable king that I am! Oh! cruel destiny that thou art!"

Perhaps, instead of accusing destiny, the king should have remembered that, as is generally the case with mankind, he was the author of his own misfortunes; for had he known how to content himself with black pudding containing a little less fat than usual, and had he abandoned his ideas of vengeance, and left dame Mousey and her family in peace beneath the hearth-stone, the affliction which he deplored would not have happened. But we must confess that the ideas of the royal father of Princess Pirlipata did not tend at all in that direction.

On the contrary—believing, as all great men do, that they must necessarily attribute their misfortunes to others—he threw all the blame upon the skilful mechanic Christian Elias Drosselmayer. Well convinced, moreover, that if he invited him back to court to be hung or beheaded, he would not accept the invitation, he desired him to come in order to receive a new order of knighthood which had just been created for men of letters, artists, and mechanics. Master Drosselmayer was not exempt from human pride: he thought that a star would look well upon the breast of his drab surtout coat; and accordingly set off for the king's court. But his joy was soon changed into fear; for on the frontiers of the kingdom, guards awaited him. They seized upon him, and conducted him from station to station, until they reached the capital.

The king, who was afraid of being won over to mercy, would not see Master Drosselmayer when the latter arrived at the palace; but he ordered him to be immediately conducted to the cradle of Pirlipata, with the assurance that if the princess were not restored by that day month to her former state of beauty, he would have the mechanic's head cut off.

Master Drosselmayer did not pretend to be bolder than his fellow-men, and had always hoped to die a natural death. He was therefore much frightened at this threat. Nevertheless, trusting a great deal to his knowledge, which his own modesty had never prevented him being aware of to its full extent, he acquired courage. Then he set to work to discover whether the evil would yield to any remedy, or whether it were really incurable, as he had from the first believed it to be.

With this object in view, he skillfully took off the head of the Princess, and next all her limbs. He likewise dissected the hands and feet, in order to examine, with more accuracy, not only the joints and the muscles, but also the internal formation. But, alas! the more he worked into the frame of Pirlipata, the more firmly did he become convinced that as the princess grew, the uglier she would become. He

therefore joined Pirlipata together again; and then, seating himself by the side of her cradle, which he was not to quit until she had resumed her former beauty, he gave way to his melancholy thoughts.

The fourth week had already commenced, and Wednesday made its appearance, when, according to custom, the king came in to see if any change had taken place in the exterior of the princess. But when he saw that it was just the same, he shook his scepter at the mechanic, crying, "Christian Elias Drosselmayer, take care of yourself! you have only three days left to restore me my daughter just as she was wont to be; and if you remain obstinate in refusing to cure her, on Monday next you shall be beheaded."

Master Drosselmayer, who could not cure the princess, not through any obstinacy on his part, but through actual ignorance how to do it, began to weep bitterly, surveying, with tearful eyes, Princess Pirlipata, who was cracking nuts as comfortably as if she were the most beautiful child upon the earth. Then as he beheld that melting spectacle, the mechanic was struck for the first time by that particular taste for nuts which the princess had shown since her birth; and he remembered also the singular fact that she was born with teeth. In fact, immediately after her change from beauty to ugliness she had begun to cry bitterly, until she found a nut near her: she had then cracked it, eaten the kernel, and turned around to sleep quietly. From that moment the nurses had taken good care to fill their pockets with nuts, and give her one or more whenever she made a face.

"Oh! instinct of nature! Eternal and mysterious sympathy of all created beings!" cried Christian Elias Drosselmayer, "thou showest me the door which leads to the discovery of thy secrets! I will knock at it, and it will open!"

At these words, which surprised the king, the mechanic turned towards his majesty and requested the favour of being conducted into the presence of the astronomer of the court. The king consented, but on condition that it should be with a guard. Master Drosselmayer would perhaps have been better pleased to take that little walk all alone; but, as under the circumstances he could not help himself, he was obliged to submit to what he could not prevent, and processed through the streets of the capital escorted like a felon.

On reaching the house of the astrologer, Master Drosselmayer threw himself into his arms; and they embraced each other amidst torrents of tears, for they were acquaintances of long standing, and were much attached to each other. They then retired to a private room, and examined a great number of books which treated upon likings and dislikings, and a host of other matters not a whit less profound. At length night came; and the astrologer ascending to his tower, and aided by Master Drosselmayer, who was himself very skilful in such matters, discovered, in spite of the difficulty of the heavenly circles which crossed each other in all directions, that in order to break the spell which rendered Princess Pirlipata hideous, and to restore her former beauty, she must eat the kernel of the Crackatook nut, the shell of which was so hard that the wheel of a forty-eight pounder might pass over it without breaking it. Moreover, it was necessary that this nut should be cracked in the presence of the princess, and by a young man who had never been shaved, and who had always worn boots. Lastly, it was requisite that he should present the nut to the princess, with his eyes closed, and in the same way step seven paces backward without stumbling. Such was the answer of the stars.

Drosselmayer and the astronomer had worked without ceasing for four days and four nights, to clear up this mysterious affair. It was on the Sunday evening—the king had finished his dinner, and was just beginning on the dessert—when the mechanic, who was to be beheaded the next day, entered the royal dining room, full of joy, and announced that he had discovered the means of restoring Princess Pirlipata to her beauty. At these news, the king caught him in his arms, with the most touching kindness, and asked him what those means were.

The mechanic thereupon explained to the king the result of his consultation with the astrologer.

"I knew perfectly well, Master Drosselmayer," said the king, "that all your delay was only through obstinacy. It is, however, settled at last; and after dinner we will set to work. Take care, then, dearest mechanic, to have the young man who has never been shaved, and who wears boots, in readiness in ten minutes, together with the nut Crackatook. Let him, moreover, abstain from drinking wine for the next hour, for fear he should stumble while walking backwards like a crab; but when once it is all over, tell him that he is welcome to my whole cellar, and may get as tipsy as he chooses."

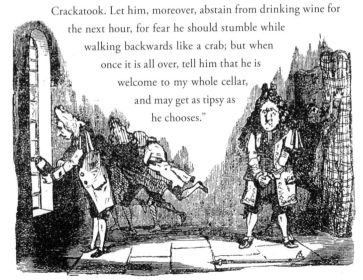

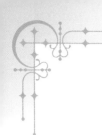

But, to the great astonishment of the king, Master Drosselmayer seemed quite frightened at these words; and, as he held his tongue, the king insisted upon knowing why he remained silent and motionless instead of hastening to execute the orders of his sovereign.

"Sire," replied the mechanician, throwing himself on his knees before the king, "it is perfectly true that we have found the means of curing Princess Pirlipata, and that those means consist of her eating a Crackatook nut when it shall have been cracked by a young man who has never been shaved, and who has always worn boots; but we have not as yet either the young man or the nut—we know not where to find them, and in all probability we shall have the greatest difficulty in discovering both the nut and the Nutcracker."

At these words, the king brandished his sceptre above the head of the mechanician, crying, "Then hasten to the scaffold!"

But the queen, on her side, hastened to kneel by the side of Master Drosselmayer, and begged her august husband to remember that by cutting off the head of the mechanician he would be losing even that ray of hope which remained to them during his lifetime; that the chances were that he who had discovered the horoscope would also find the nut and the Nutcracker; that they ought to believe more firmly in the present prediction of the astronomer, inasmuch as nothing which he had hitherto prophesied had ever come to pass,

but that it was evident his presages must be fulfilled some day or another; inasmuch as the king had named him his grand prophet; and that, as the princess was not yet of an age to marry (she being now only three months old), and would not even be marriageable until she was fifteen, there was consequently a period of fourteen years and nine months during which Master Drosselmayer and the astrologer might search after the Crackatook nut and the young man who was to break it. The queen therefore suggested that a reprieve might be awarded to Christian Elias Drosselmayer, at the expiration of which he should return to surrender himself into the king's power, whether he had found the means of curing the princess, or not; and either to be generously rewarded, or put to death without mercy.

The king, who was a very just man, and who on that day especially had dined splendidly upon his two favourite dishes—namely, liver soup and black puddings—lent a favourable ear to the prayer of his wise and courageous queen. He therefore decided that the astrologer and the mechanician should that moment set out in search of the nut and the Nutcracker; for which purpose he granted fourteen years and nine months, with the condition that they should return, at the expiration of that reprieve, to place themselves in his power, so that, if they were empty-handed, he might deal with them according to his own royal pleasure.

If, on the contrary, they should make their reappearance with the Crackatook nut which was to restore the princess to all her former beauty, the astrologer would be rewarded with a yearly pension of six hundred pounds and a telescope of honour; and the mechanician would receive a sword set with diamonds, the Order of the Golden Spider (the grand order of the state), and new frock-coat.

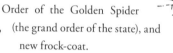

As for the young man who was to crack the nut, the king had no doubt of being able to find one suitable for the purpose, by means of advertisements constantly inserted in the national and foreign newspapers.

Touched by this declaration on the part of the king, which relieved them from half the difficulty of their task, Christian Elias Drosselmayer pledged his honour that he would either find the Cracktook-nut, or return, like another Regulus, to place himself in the hands of the king.

That same evening the astrologer and the mechanician departed from the capital of the kingdom to commence their researches.

* * * * *

How The Mechanician and The Astrologer Wander Over The Four Quarters of The World, and Discover a Fifth, Without Finding The Crackatook Nut

It was now fourteen years and five months since the astrologer and the mechanician first set out on their wanderings through all parts, without discovering a vestige of what they sought. They had first of all travelled through Europe; then they visited America, next Africa, and afterwards Asia: they even discovered a fifth part of the world, which learned men have since called New Holland, because it was discovered by two Germans! But throughout that long series of travels, although they had seen many nuts of different shapes and sizes, they never fell in with the Crackatook nut. They had, however, in alas! a vain hope, passed several years at the court of the King of Dates and at that of the Prince of Almonds: they had uselessly consulted the celebrated Academy of Grau Monkeys and the famous Naturalist Society of Squirrels; until at length they arrived, sinking with fatigue, upon the borders of the great forest which touches the feet of the Himalayan Mountains. And now they dolefully said to each other that they had only a hundred and twenty-two days to find what they sought, after a useless search of fourteen years and five months.

If I were to tell you, my dear children, the strange adventures which happened to the two travelers during that long wandering, I should occupy you every evening for an entire month, and should then weary you in the long run. I will therefore only tell you that Christian Elias Drosselmayer, who was the most eager in search after the nut,—since his head depended upon finding it,—gave himself up to greater dangers than his companion, and lost all his hair by a stroke of the sun received in the tropics. He also lost his right eye by an arrow which a Caribbean Chief aimed at him. Moreover, his drab frock-coat, which was not new when he left Germany, had literally fallen into rags and tatters. His situation was therefore most deplorable; and yet, so much do men cling to life, that, damaged as he was by the various accidents which had befallen him, he beheld with increasing terror the approach of the moment when he must return to place himself in the power of the king.

Nevertheless, the mechanician was a man of honour: he would not break a promise so sacred as that which he had made. He

accordingly resolved, whatever might happen, to set out the very next morning on his return to Germany. And indeed there was no time to lose; fourteen years and five months had passed away, and the two travelers had only a hundred and twenty-two days, as we have already said, to reach the capital of Princess Pirlipata's father.

Christian Elias Drosselmayer accordingly made known his noble intention to his friend the astrologer; and both decided that they would set out on their return the next morning.

And, true to this intention, the travelers resumed their journey at daybreak, taking the direction of Bagdad. From Bagdad they proceeded to Alexandria, where they embarked for Venice. From Venice they passed through the Tyrol; and from the Tyrol they entered into the kingdom of Pirlipata's father, both sincerely hoping that he was either dead or in his dotage.

But, alas! it was no such thing! Upon reaching the capital, the unfortunate mechanician learnt that the worthy monarch not only had not lost his intellectual faculties, but was also in better health than ever. There was consequently no chance for him—unless Princess Pirlipata had become cured of her ugliness without any remedy at all, which was not possible; or, that the king's heart had softened, which was not probable—of escaping the dreadful fate which threatened him.

He did not however present himself the less boldly at the gate of the palace, for he was sustained by the idea that he was doing an heroic action; and he accordingly desired to speak to the king.

The king, who was of easy access, and who gave an audience to whomsoever he had business with, ordered the grand master of the ceremonies to bring the strangers into his presence.

The grand master of the ceremonies then stated that the strangers were of a most villainous appearance, and could not possibly be worse dressed. But the king answered that it was wrong to judge the heart by the countenance, and the gown did not make the parson.

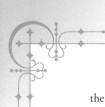

Thereupon, the grand master of the ceremonies, having perceived the correctness of these observations, bowed respectfully and proceeded to fetch the mechanician and the astrologer.

The king was the same as ever, and they immediately recognised him; but the travellers were so changed, especially poor Elias Drosselmayer, that they were obliged to declare who they were.

Upon seeing the two travellers return of their own accord, the king gave a sign of joy, for he felt convinced that they would not have come back if they had not found the Crackatook nut. But he was speedily undeceived; and the mechanician, throwing himself at his feet, confessed that, in spite of the most earnest and constant search, his friend and himself had returned empty-handed.

The king, as we have said, although of a passionate disposition, was an excellent man at bottom; he was touched by the punctuality with which Christian Elias Drosselmayer had kept his word; and he changed the sentence of death, long before pronounced against him, into imprisonment for life. As for the astrologer, he contented himself by banishing that great sage.

But as three days were still remaining of the period of fourteen years and nine months' delay, granted by the king, Master Drosselmayer, who was deeply attached to his country, implored the king's permission to profit by those three days to visit Nuremberg once more.

This request seemed so just to the king, that he granted it without any restriction.

Master Drosselmayer, having only three days left, resolved to profit by that time as much as possible; and, having fortunately found that two places in the mail were not taken, he secured them that moment.

Now, as the astrologer was himself condemned to banishment,

and as it was all the same to him which way he went, he took his departure with the mechanician.

Next morning, at about ten o'clock, they were at Nuremberg. As Master Drosselmayer had only one relation in the world, namely his brother, Christopher Zacharias Drosselmayer, who kept one of the principal toy-shops in Nuremberg, it was at his house that he alighted.

Christopher Zacharias Drosselmayer was overjoyed to see his poor brother Christian Elias, whom he had believed to be dead. In the first instance he would not admit that the man with the bald head and the black patch upon the eye was in reality his brother; but the mechanician showed him his famous drab surtout coat, which, all tattered as it was, had retained in certain parts some traces of its original colour; and in support of that first proof he mentioned so many family secrets, unknown to all save Zacharias and himself, that the toy-merchant was compelled to yield to the evidence brought forward.

He then inquired of him what had kept him so long absent from his native city, and in what country he had left his hair, his eye, and the missing pieces of his coat.

Christian Elias Drosselmayer had no motive to keep secret from his brother the events which had occurred. He began by introducing his companion in misfortune; and, this formal usage having been performed, he related his adventures from A to Z, ending them by saying that he had only a few hours to stay with his brother, because, not having found the Crackatook nut, he was on the point of being shut up in a dungeon forever.

While Christian Elias was telling his story, Christopher Zacharias had more than once twiddled his finger and thumb, turned round upon one leg, and made a certain knowing noise with his tongue. Under any other circumstances, the mechanician would have demanded of him what those signs meant; but he was so full of thought, that he saw nothing; and it was only when his brother exclaimed, "Hem! Hem!" twice, and "Oh! oh! oh!" three times, that he asked the reason of those expressions.

"The reason is," said Christopher Zacharias, "that it would be strange indeed if—but, no—and yet—"

"What do you mean?" cried the mechanician.

"If—" continued the toy merchant.

"If what?" again said Master Drosselmayer.

But instead of giving any answer, Christopher Zacharias, who, during those short questions and answers, had no doubt collected his thoughts, threw his wig up into the air, and began to caper about, crying, "Brother, you are saved! You shall not go to prison; for either I am much mistaken, or I myself am in possession of the Crackatook nut."

And, without giving any further explanation to his astonished brother, Christopher Zacharias rushed out of the room, but returned in a moment with a box containing a large gilt filbert, which he presented to the mechanician.

The mechanician, who dared not believe in such good luck, took the nut with hesitation, and turned it round in all directions so as to examine it with the attention which it deserved. He then declared that he was of the same opinion as his brother, and that he should be much astonished if that filbert were not indeed the Crackatook nut. Thus saying, he handed it to the astrologer, and asked his opinion.

The astrologer examined it with as much attention as Master Drosselmayer had done; but shaking his head, he replied, "I should also be of the same opinion as yourself and brother, if the nut were not gilt; but I have not seen anything in the stars showing that the nut we are in search of ought to be so ornamented. Besides, how came your brother by the Crackatook nut?"

"I will explain the whole thing to you," said Christopher, "and tell you how the nut fell into my hands, and how it came to have gilding which prevents you from recognising it, and which indeed is not its own naturally."

Then—having made them sit down, for he very wisely thought that after travelling for fourteen years and nine months they must be tired—he began as follows:

"The very day on which the king sent for you under pretence of giving you an Order of Knighthood, a stranger arrived at Nuremberg, carrying with him a bag of nuts which he had to sell. But the nut merchants of this town, being anxious to keep the monopoly themselves, quarrelled with him just opposite my shop. The stranger,

with a view to defend himself more easily, placed his bag of nuts upon the ground, and the fight continued, to the great delight of the little boys and the ticket-porters; when a waggon, heavily laden, passed over the bag of nuts. Upon seeing this accident, which they attributed to the justice of heaven, the merchants considered that they were sufficiently avenged, and left the stranger alone. He picked up his bag, and all his nuts were found to be cracked, save ONE—one only—which he handed to me with a strange kind of smile requesting me to buy it for a new zwanziger of the year 1720, and declaring that the day would come when I should not repent the bargain, dear as it might seem. I felt in my pocket, and was much surprised to find a zwanziger of the kind mentioned by this man. The coincidence seemed so strange, that I gave him my zwanziger; he handed me the nut, and I took his departure.

"I placed the nut in my window for sale; and although I only asked two kreutzers more than the money I had given for it, it remained in the window for seven or eight years without finding a purchaser. I then had it gilt to increase its value; but for that purpose I uselessly

spent two zwanzigers more; for the nut has been here ever since the day I bought it."

At that moment the astrologer, in whose hands the nut had remained, uttered a cry of joy. While Master Drosselmayer was listening to his brother's story, the astrologer had delicately scraped off some of the gilding of the nut; and on the shell he had found the word "Crackatook" engraven in Chinese characters.

All doubts were now cleared up; and the three individuals danced for joy, the real Crackatook nut being actually in their possession.

* * * * *

How, After Having Found The Crackatook Nut, The Mechanician And The Astrologer Find The Young Man Who Is To Crack It

Christian Elias Drosselmayer was in such a hurry to announce the good news to the king, that he was anxious to return by the mail that very moment; but Christian Zecharias begged him to stay at least until his soon should come in. The mechanician yielded the more easily to this request, because he had not seen his nephew for fifteen years, and because, on recalling the idea of the past, he remembered that at the time when he quitted Nuremberg, he had left the said nephew a fine fat romping fellow of only three and a half, but of whom he (the uncle) was doatingly fond.

While he was thinking of these things, a handsome young man of between eighteen and nineteen entered the shop of Christopher Zacharias, whom he saluted by the name of "Father." Then Christopher Zacharias, having embraced him, presented him to Christian Elias, saying to the young man, "And now embrace your uncle."

The young man hesitated; for Uncle Drosselmayer, with his frock-coat in rags, his bald head, and the plaster upon his eye, did not seem a very inviting person. But his father observed the hesitation, and as he was fearful that Christian Elias's feelings would be wounded, he pushed his son forward, and thrust him into the arms of the mechanician.

In the meantime the astrologer had kept his eyes fixed upon the young man with a steady attention which seemed so singular that the youth felt ill at his ease in being so stared at, and left the room.

The astrologer then put several questions to Christopher Zecharias concerning his son; and the father answered them with all the enthusiasm of a fond parent.

Young Drosselmayer was, as his appearance indicated, between seventeen and eighteen. From his earliest years he had been so funny and yet so tractable, that his mother had taken a delight in dressing him like some of the puppets which her husband sold: namely, sometimes as a student, sometimes as a postilion, sometimes as a Hungarian, but always in a garb that required boots; because, as he possessed the prettiest little foot in the world, but had a rather small calf, the boots showed off the little foot, and concealed the fault of the calf.

"And so," said the astrologer to Christopher Zecharias, "your son has always worn boots?"

Christian Elias now stared in his turn.

"My son has never worn anything but boots," replied the toy-man. "At the age of ten," he continued, "I sent him to the university of

Tubingen, where he remained till he was eighteen, without contracting any of the bad habits of his companions, such as drinking, swearing, and fighting. The only weakness of which I believe him to be guilty, is that he allows the four or five wretched hairs which he has upon his chin to grow, without permitting a barber to touch his countenance.

"And thus," said the astrologer, "your son has never been shaved?"

Christian Elias stared more and more.

"Never," answered Christopher Zecharias.

"And during the holidays," continued the astrologer, "how did he pass his time?"

"Why," replied the father, "he used to remain in the shop, in his becoming student's dress; and, through pure good-nature, he cracked nuts for all the young ladies who came to the shop to buy toys and who, on that account, called him *Nutcracker*."

"Nutcracker!" cried the mechanician.

"Nutcracker!" repeated the astrologer in his turn.

And then they looked at each other while Christopher Zecharias looked at them both.

"My dear sir," said the astrologer to the toy-man, "in my opinion your fortune is as good as made."

The toy-man, who had not heard this prophecy without a feeling of pleasure, required an explanation, which the astrologer, however, put off until the next morning.

When the mechanician and the astrologer were shown to their apartment, and were alone together, the astrologer embraced his friend, crying, "It is he! We have him!"

"Do you think so?" demanded Christian Elias, in the tone of a man who had his doubts, but who only wished to be convinced.

"Can there be any uncertainty?" exclaimed the astrologer: "he has all the necessary qualifications!"

"Let us sum them up."

"He has never warn anything but boots."

"True!"

"He has never been shaved."

"True, again!"

"And through good-nature, he has stood in his father's shop to crack nuts for young persons, who never called him by any other name than *Nutcracker*."

"All this is quite true."

"My dear friend," added the astrologer, "one stroke of good luck never comes alone. But if you still doubt, let us go and consult the stars."

They accordingly ascended to the roof of the house; and, having drawn the young man's horoscope, discovered that he was intended for great things.

This prophecy, which confirmed all the astrologer's hopes, forced the mechanician to adopt his opinion.

"And now," said the astrologer, in a triumphant tone, "there are only two things which we must not neglect."

"What are they?" demanded Christian Elias.

"The first, is that you must fit to the nape of your nephew's neck a large piece of wood, which must be so well connected to the lower jaw that it will increase its power by the fact of pressure."

"Nothing is more easy," answered Christian Elias; "it is the A, B, C of mechanics."

"The second thing," continued the astrologer, "is, that on arriving at the residence of the king, we must carefully conceal the fact that we have brought with us the young man who is destined to crack the Crackatook nut. For my opinion is that the more teeth there are broken, and the more jaws there are dislocated in trying to break the Crackatook nut, the more eager the king will be to offer a great reward to whim who shall succeed where so many have failed."

"My dear friend," answered the mechanician, "you are a man of sound sense. Let us go to bed."

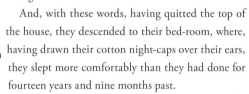

And, with these words, having quitted the top of the house, they descended to their bed-room, where, having drawn their cotton night-caps over their ears, they slept more comfortably than they had done for fourteen years and nine months past.

On the following morning, at an early hour, the two friends went down to the apartment of Christopher Zecharias, and told him all the fine plans they had formed the evening before. Now, as the toyman was not wanting in ambition, and as, in his paternal fondness, he fancied that his son must certainly possess the strongest jaws in all Germany, he gladly assented to the arrangement, which was to take from his shop not only the nut but also the *Nutcracker.*

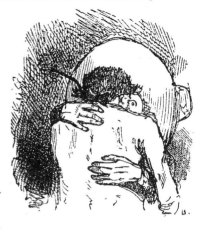

The young man himself was more difficult to persuade. The wooden counter-balance which it was proposed to fix to the back of his neck, instead of the pretty little tie which kept his hair in such neat folds, particularly vexed him. But his father, his uncle, and the astrologer made him such splendid promises, that he consented. Christian Elias Drosselmayer, therefore, went to work that moment; the wooden balance was soon made; and it was strongly fixed to the nape of the young man now so full of hope. Let me also state, to satisfy your curiosity, that the contrivance worked so well that on the very first the skilful mechanician received brilliant proofs of his success, for the young man was enabled to crack the hardest apricot-stones, and the most obstinate peach-stones.

These trials having been made, the astrologer, the mechanician, and young Drosselmayer set out immediately for the king's dwellings. Christopher Zecharias was anxious to go with them; but, as he was forced to take care of his shop, that excellent father resigned himself to necessity, and remained behind at Nuremberg.

* * * * *

The mechanician, on reaching the capital, took good care to leave young Drosselmayer at the inn where they put up. They then proceeded to the palace to announce that having vainly sought the Crackatook nut all over the world, they had at length found it at Nuremberg. But of him who was to crack it, they said not a word, according to the arrangement made between them.

The joy at the palace was very great. The king sent directly for the privy councilor who had the care of the public mind, and who acted as censor in respect to the newspapers; and this great man, by the king's command, drew up an article to be inserted in the *Royal Gazette*, and which all other newspapers were ordered to copy, to the effect that *"all persons who fancied that they had teeth good enough to break the Crackatook nut, were to present themselves at the palace, and if they succeeded, would be liberally rewarded for their trouble."*

This circumstance was well-suited to show how rich the kingdom was in strong jaws. The candidates were so numerous, that the king was forced to form a jury, the foreman of whom was the crown dentist; and their duty was to examine all the competitors, to see if they had all their thirty-two teeth perfect, and whether any were decayed.

Three thousand five hundred candidates were admitted to this first trial, which lasted a week, and which produced only an immense number of broken teeth and jaws out of place.

It was therefore necessary to make a second appeal; and all the national and foreign newspapers were crammed with advertisements to that purpose. The king offered the post of Perpetual President of the Academy, and the Order of the Golden Spider to whomsoever should succeed in cracking the Crackatook nut. There was no necessity to have a degree of Doctor of Philosophy, or Master of Arts, to be competent to stand as a candidate.

This second trial produced five thousand candidates. All the learned societies of Europe sent deputies to this important assembly. Several members of the English Royal Society were present; and a great number of critics belonging to the leading London newspapers and literary journals; but they were not able to stand as candidates, because their teeth had all been broken long before in their frequent attempts to tear to pieces the works of their brother authors. This second trial, which lasted a fortnight, was, alas! as fruitless as the first. The

deputies of the learned societies disputed amongst themselves, for the honour of the association to which they respectively belonged, as to who should break the nut; but they only left their best teeth behind them.

As for the nut itself, its shell did not even bear the marks of the attempts that had been made to crack it.

The king was in despair. He resolved, however, to strike one grand blow; and, as he had no male descendant, he declared, by means of a third article in the *Royal Gazette*, the national newspapers, and the foreign journals, that the hand of Princess Pirlipata and the inheritance of the throne should be given to him who might crack the Crackatook nut. There was one condition to this announcement; namely, that this time the candidates must be from sixteen to twenty-four years of age. The promise of such a reward excited all Germany. Competitors poured in from all parts of Europe; and they would even have come from Asia, Africa, and America, and that fifth quarter of the world which had been discovered by Christian Elias Drosselmayer and his friend the astrologer,

if there had been sufficient time.

On this occasion the mechanician and the astrologer thought that the moment was now come to produce young Drosselmayer; for it was impossible for the king to offer a higher reward than that just announced. Only, certain of success

as they were, and although this time a host of princes and royal and imperial jaws had presented themselves, the mechanism and the astronomer did not appear with their young friend at the register-office until just as it was about to close; so that the name NATHANIEL DROSSELMAYER was number the 11,375th, and stood last.

It was on this occasion as on the preceding ones. The 11,374 rivals of young Drosselmayer were foiled; and on the nineteenth day of the trial, at twenty-five minutes to twelve o'clock, and just as the princess accomplished her fifteenth year, the name of Nathaniel Drosselmayer was called.

The young man presented himself, accompanied by his two guardians, the mechanician and the astrologer. It was the first time

that these two illustrious persons had seen the princess since they had beheld her in the cradle; and since that period great changes had taken place with her. But I must inform you, with due candour, that those changes were not to her advantage. When a child, she was shockingly ugly: she was now frightfully so.

Her form had lost, with its growth, none of its important features. It is therefore difficult to understand how those skinny legs, those flat hips, and that distorted body, could have supported such a monstrous head. And that head had the same grizzled hair—the same green eyes—the same enormous mouth—and the same cotton beard on the chin, as we have already described; only all these features were just fifteen years older.

Upon perceiving that monster of ugliness, poor Nathaniel shuddered and inquired of the mechanician and the astrologer if they were quite sure that the kernel of the Crackatook nut would restore the princess to her beauty: because, if she were to remain in that state, he was quite willing to make the trial in a matter where all the others had failed; but he should leave the honour of the marriage and the profit of the heirship of the throne to any one who might be inclined to accept them. It is hardly necessary to state that both the mechanician and the astrologer reassured their young friend, promising that the nut, once broke, and the kernel, once eaten, Pirlipata would become that very moment the most beautiful princess on the face of the earth.

But if the sight of Princess Pirlipata had struck poor Nathaniel with dismay, I must tell you, in honour of the young man, that *his* presence had produced a very different effect upon the sensitive heart of the heiress of the crown; and she could not prevent herself from exclaiming, when she saw him, "Oh! how glad I should be if he were to break the nut!"

Thereupon the chief governess of the princess replied, "I think I have often observed to your highness, that it is not customary for a young and beautiful princess like yourself to express her opinion aloud relative to such matters."

Nathaniel was indeed calculated to turn the heads of all the princesses in the world. He wore a little military frock-coat, of a violet colour, all braided, and with golden buttons, and which his uncle had made for this solemn occasion. His breeches were of

the same stuff; and his boots were so well blacked, and sat in such admirable manner, that they seemed as if they were painted. The only thing which somewhat spoilt his appearance was the ugly piece of wood fitted to the nape of his neck; but Uncle Drosselmayer had so contrived that it seemed like a little bag attached to his wig, and might at a stretch have passed as an eccentricity of the toilet, or else as a new fashion which Nathaniel's tailor was trying to push into vogue at the court.

Thus it was, that when this charming young man entered the great hall, what the princess had the imprudence to say aloud, the other ladies present said to themselves; and there was not a person, not even excepting the king and the queen, who did not desire at the bottom of his heart that Nathaniel might prove triumphant in the adventure which he had undertaken.

On his side, young Drosselmayer approached with a confidence which encouraged the hopes that were placed in him. Having reached the steps leading to the throne, he bowed to the king and queen, then to Princess Pirlipata, and then to the spectators; after which he received the Crackatook nut from the grand master of the ceremonies, took it delicately between his fore-finger and thumb, placed it in his mouth, and gave a violent pull at the wooden balance hanging behind him.

Crack! crack!—and the shell was broken in several pieces.

He then skilfully detached the kernel from the fibres hanging to it, and presented it to the princess, bowing gracefully but respectfully at the same time; after which he closed his eyes, and began to walk backwards. At the same moment the princess swallowed the kernel; and, O! wonder! her horrible ugliness disappeared, and she became a young lady of angelic beauty. Her face seemed to have borrowed the hues of the rose and the lily: her eyes were of sparkling azure; and thick tresses, resembling masses of golden thread, flowed over her alabaster shoulders.

The trumpets and the cymbals sounded enough to make one deaf; and the shouts of the people responded to the noise of the instruments. The king, the ministers, the councillors of state, and the judges began to dance, as they had done at the birth of Pirlipata; and eau-de-cologne was obliged to be thrown in the face of the queen, who had fainted for joy.

The great tumult proved very annoying to young Nathaniel Drosselmayer, who, as you must remember, had yet to step seven paces backwards. He, however, behaved with a coolness which gave the highest hopes relative to the period when he should be called upon to reign in his turn; and he was just stretching out his leg to take the seventh step, when the queen of the mice suddenly appeared through a crevice in the floor. With horrible squeaks she ran between his legs; so that just at that very moment when the future Prince Royal placed his foot upon the ground, his heel came so fully on the body of the mouse that he stumbled in such a manner as to nearly fall.

O sorrow! At the same instant the handsome young man became as ugly as the princess was before him; his shrunken form could hardly support his enormous head; his eyes became green, haggard, and goggle; his mouth split from ear to ear; and his delicate little sprouting beard changed into a white and soft substance, which was afterward found to be cotton.

But the cause of this event was punished at the same moment that she produced it. Dame Mousey was weltering in her own blood upon the floor. Her wickedness did not therefore go without its punishment. In fact, young Drosselmayer had trampled so hard upon her with his heel, that she was crushed beyond all hope of recovery. But, while still writing on the floor, Dame Mousey squeaked forth the following words, with all the strength of her agonizing voice:

> "Crackatook! Crackatook! fatal nut that thou art,
> Through thee has Death reached me, at length, with his
> dart!
> > Heigho! heigho!
> But the Queen of the Mice has thousands to back her,
> And my son will yet punish that wretched Nutcracker,
> > I know! I know!

> "Sweet life, adieu!
> > Too soon snatch'd away!
> And thou heaven of blue,
> > And thou world so gay,
> Adieu! adieu!"

The verses of Dame Mousey might have been better; but one cannot be very correct, as you will all agree, when breathing the last sigh!

And when that last sigh was rendered, a great officer of the court took up Dame Mousey by the tail, and carried her away for the purpose of interring her remains in the hole where so many of her family had been buried fifteen years and some months beforehand.

As, in the middle of all this, no one had troubled themselves about Nathaniel Drosselmayer except the mechanician and the astrologer, the princess, who was unaware of the accident which had happened, ordered the young hero to be brought into her presence; for, in spite of the lesson read to her by the governess, she was in haste to thank him. But scarcely had she perceived the unfortunate Nathaniel, than she hid her face in her hands; and, forgetting the service which he had rendered her, cried, "Turn out the horrible Nutcracker! turn him out! turn him out!"

The grand marshal of the palace accordingly took poor Nathaniel by the shoulders and pushed him down stairs. The king, who was very angry at having a Nutcracker proposed to him as his son-in-law, attacked the astrologer and the mechanician; and, instead of the income of six hundred pounds a year and the telescope of honour which he had promised the first—instead, also, of the sword set with diamonds, the Order of the Golden Spider, and the drab frock-coat, which he ought to have given the latter—he banished them both from his kingdom, granting them only twenty-four hours to cross the frontiers.

Obedience was necessary. The mechanician, the astrologer, and young Drosselmayer (now become a Nutcracker), left the capital and quitted the country. But when night came, the two learned men consulted the stars once more, and read in them that, all deformed though he were, Nathaniel would not the less become a prince and

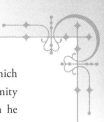

king, unless indeed he chose to remain a private individual, which was left to his own choice. This was to happen when his deformity should disappear; and that deformity would disappear when he should have commanded an army in battle—when he should have killed the seven-headed king of the mice, who was born after Dame Mousey's seven first sons had been put to death—and, lastly, when a beautiful lady should fall in love with him.

But while awaiting these brilliant destinies, Nathaniel Drosselmayer, who had left the paternal shop as the only son and heir, now returned to it in the form of a Nutcracker!

I need scarcely tell you that his father did not recognise him; and that, when Christopher Zacharias inquired of the mechanician and his friend the astrologer, what had become of his dearly-beloved son, those two illustrious persons replied, with the seriousness of learned men, that the king and the queen would not allow the saviour of the princess to leave them, and that young Nathaniel remained at court covered with honour and glory. As for the unfortunate Nutcracker, who felt how deeply painful was his situation, he uttered not a word, but resolved to await patiently the change which must some day or another take place in him. Nevertheless, I must candidly admit, that in spite of the good nature of his disposition, he was desperately vexed with Uncle Drosselmayer, who, coming at a moment he was so little expected, and having enticed him away by so many fine promises, was the sole and only cause of the frightful misfortune that had occurred to him.

Such, my dear children, is the History of the Crackatook Nut, just as Godfather Drosselmayer told it to little Mary and Fritz; and you can now understand why people often say, when speaking of anything difficult to do, "That is a hard nut to crack."

* * * * *

The Uncle and the Nephew

If any one of my young friends now around me has ever cut himself with glass, which he has most likely done in the days of his disobedience, he must know by experience that it is a particularly disagreeable kind of cut, because it is so long in healing. Mary was, therefore, forced to stay a whole week in bed; for she always felt giddy whenever she tried to get up. But at last she got well altogether, and was able to skip about the room as she was wont to do.

You would not do my little heroine the injustice to suppose that her first visit was to any other place than the glass cupboard, which now seemed quite charming to look at. A new pane had been put in; and all the windows had been so well cleaned by Miss Trudchen, that all the trees, houses, dolls, and other toys of the Christmas eve seemed quite new, gay, and polished. But in the midst of all the treasures of her little kingdom, and before all other things, Mary perceived her Nutcracker smiling upon her from the second shelf where he was placed, and with his teeth all in as good order as ever they were. While thus joyfully examining her favourite, an idea which had more than once presented itself to the mind of Mary touched her to the quick. She was persuaded that all Godfather Drosselmayer had told her was not a mere fable, but the true history of the disagreement between the Nutcracker on one side, and the late queen of the mice and her son, the reigning king, on the other side. She, therefore, knew that the Nutcracker could be neither more nor less than Nathaniel Drosselmayer, of Nuremberg, the amiable but enchanted nephew of her godfather; for that the skilful mechanician who had figured at the court of Pirlipata's father, was Doctor Drosselmayer, she had never doubted from the moment when he introduced his drab frock-coat into his tale. This belief was strengthened when she found him losing first his hair by a sun-stroke, and then his eye by an arrow, events which had rendered necessary the invention of the ugly black patch, and of the ingenious glass wig, of which I have already spoken.

"But why did not your uncle help you, poor Nutcracker?" said Mary, as she stood at the glass cupboard, gazing up at her favourite; for she remembered that on the success of the battle depended the disenchantment of the poor little man and his elevation to the rank of king of the kingdom of toys. Then she thought that all the dolls, puppets, and little men must be well prepared to receive him as their king; for did they not obey the Nutcracker as soldiers obey a general? That indifference on the part of Godfather Drosselmayer was so much the more annoying to little Mary, because she was certain that those dolls and puppets to which, in her imagination, she gave life and motion, really did live and move.

Nevertheless, there was now no appearance of either life or motion in the cupboard, where everything was still and quiet. But Mary, rather than give up her sincere belief, thought that all this was occasioned by the sorcery of the late queen of the mice and her son; and so firm was she in this belief, that, while she gazed up at the Nutcracker, she continued to say aloud what she had only begun to say to herself.

"And yet," she resumed, "although you are unable to move, and are prevented by enchantment from saying a single word to me, I am very sure, my dear Mr. Drosselmayer, that you understand me perfectly, and that you are well aware of my good intentions with regard to you. Reckon, then, upon my support when you require it; and in the meantime, do not vex yourself. I will go straight to your uncle, and beg him to assist you; and if he only loves you a little, he is so clever that I am sure he can help you."

In spite of the eloquence of this speech, the Nutcracker did not move an inch; but it seemed to Mary that a sigh came from behind the glass, the panes of which began to sound very low, but wonderfully soft and pleasing; while it appeared to Mary that a sweet voice, like a small silver bell, said, "Dear little Mary, thou art my guardian angel! I will be thine, and Mary shall be mine!" And at these words, so mysteriously heard, Mary felt a singular sensation of happiness, in spite of the shudder which passed through her entire frame.

Twilight had now arrived; and the judge returned home, accompanied by Doctor Drosselmayer. In a few moments Miss Trudchen got tea ready, and all the family were gathered round the table, talking gaily. As for Mary, she had been to fetch her little arm-chair, and had seated herself in silence at the feet of Godfather Drosselmayer. Taking advantage of a moment when no one was speaking, she raised her large blue eyes towards the doctor, and, looking earnestly at him, said, "I now know, dear godpapa, that my Nutcracker is your nephew, young Drosselmayer, of Nuremberg. He has become a prince, and also a king of the kingdom of toys, as your friend the astrologer prophesied. But you know that he is at open war with the king of the mice. Come, dear godpapa, tell me why you did not help him when you were sitting astride upon the clock? and why do you now desert him?"

And, with these words, Mary again related, amidst the laughter of her father, her mother, and Miss Trudchen, the events of that famous battle which she had seen. Fritz and Godfather Drosselmayer alone did not enjoy the whole scene.

"Where," said the godfather, "does that little girl get all those foolish ideas which enter her head?"

"She has a very lively imagination," replied Mary's mother; "and, after all, these are only dreams and visions occasioned by fever."

"And I can prove *that*," shouted Fritz; "for she says that my red hussars took to flight, which cannot possibly be true—unless indeed they are abominable cowards, in which case they would not get the better of me, for I would flog them all soundly."

Then, with a singular smile, Godfather Drosselmayer took Mary upon his knees, and said with more kindness than before, "My dear child, you do not know what course you are pursuing in espousing so warmly the cause of your Nutcracker. You will have to suffer much if you persist in taking the part of one who is in disgrace; for the king of the mice, who considers him to be the murderer of his mother, will persecute him in all ways. But, in any case, remember that it is not I—but you alone—who can save him. Be firm and faithful—and all will go well."

Neither Mary nor anyone else understood the words of Godfather Drosselmayer: on the contrary, those words seemed so strange to the judge, that he took the doctor's hand, felt his pulse for some moments in silence, and then said, "My dear friend, you are very feverish, and I should advise you to go home to bed."

The Duel

During the night, which followed the scene just related, and while the moon, shining in all its splendour, cast its bright rays through the openings in the curtains, Mary, who now slept with her mother, was awakened by a noise that seemed to come from the corner of the room, and was mingled with sharp screeches and squeakings.

"Alas!" cried Mary, who remembered to have heard the same noise on the occasion of the famous battle; "alas! the mice are coming again! Mamma, mamma, mamma!"

But her voice was stifled in her throat, in spite of all her efforts: she endeavoured to get up to run out of the room, but seemed to be nailed to her bed, unable to move her limbs. At length, turning her affrighted eyes towards the corner of the room, when the noise came, she beheld the king of the mice scraping for himself a way through the wall, and thrusting in first one of his heads, then another, then a third, and so on until the whole seven, each with a crown, made their appearance. Having entered the room, he walked several times round it like a victor who takes possession of his conquest: he then leapt with one bound upon a table that was standing near the bed. Gazing upon her with his fourteen eyes, all as bright as carbuncles, and with a gnashing of his teeth and a horrible squeaking noise, he said, "Fe, fa, fum! You must give me all your sugar-plums and your sweet cakes, little girl, and if not, I will eat up your friend the Nutcracker."

Then, having uttered this threat, he fled from the room by the same hole as he had entered by.

Mary was so frightened by this terrible apparition, that she awoke in the morning very pale and broken-hearted, the more so that she dared not mention what had taken place during the night, for fear of being laughed at. Twenty times was she on the point of telling all, either to her mother or to Fritz; but she stopped, still thinking that neither the one nor the other would believe her. It was, however, pretty clear that she must sacrifice her sugar-plums and her sweet cakes to the safety of the poor Nutcracker. She accordingly placed them all on the ledge of the cupboard that very evening.

Next morning, the judge's wife said, "I really do not know whence come all the mice that have suddenly invaded the house; but those naughty creatures have actually eaten up all my poor little Mary's sugar-plums."

The lady was not quite right; the sugar-plums and cakes were only *spoilt*, not *eaten up*; for the gluttonous king of the mice, not finding the sweet cakes as good as he expected, messed them about so that they were forced to be thrown away.

But as it was not sugar-plums that Mary liked best, she did not feel much regret at the sacrifice which the king of the mice had extorted from her; and, thinking that he would be content with the first contribution with which he had taxed her, she was much pleased at the idea of having saved Nutcracker upon such good terms.

Unfortunately her satisfaction was not of long duration; for the following night she was again awoke by hearing squeaking and whining close by her ears.

Alas! it was the king of the mice again, his eyes shining more horribly than on the preceding night; and, in a voice interrupted by frequent whines and squeaks, he said, "You must give me your little sugar dolls and figures made of biscuit, little girl; if not, I will eat up your friend the Nutcracker."

Thereupon the king of the mice went skipping away, and disappeared by the hole in the wall.

Next morning, Mary, now deeply afflicted, went straight to the glass cupboard, and threw a mournful look upon her figures of sugar and biscuit; and her grief was very natural, for never were such nice-looking sweet things seen before.

"Alas!" she said, as she turned towards the Nutcracker, "what would I not do for you, my dear Mr. Drosselmayer? But you must admit all the same that what I am required to do is very hard."

At these words the Nutcracker assumed so piteous an air, that Mary, who fancied that she was for ever beholding the jaws of the king of the mice opening to devour him, resolved to make this second sacrifice to save the unfortunate young man. That very evening, therefore, she placed her sugar figures and her biscuits upon the ledge of the cupboard, where the night before she had put her sugar-plums and sweet cakes. Kissing them, however, one after another, as a token of farewell, she yielded up her shepherds and shepherdesses, and her sheep, concealing behind the flock at the same time a little sugar baby with fat round cheeks, and which she loved above all the other things.

"Now really this is too bad!" cried the judge's wife next morning: "it is very clear that these odious mice have taken up their dwelling in the glass cupboard; for all poor Mary's sugar figures are eaten up."

At these words large tears started from Mary's eyes; but she dried them up almost directly, and even smiled sweetly as she thought to herself, "What matter my shepherds, shepherdesses, and sheep, since the Nutcracker is saved!"

"Mamma," cried Fritz, who was present at the time, "I must remind you that our baker has an excellent grey cat, which we might send for, and which would soon put an end to all this by snapping up the mice one after another, and even Dame Mousey herself afterwards, as well as her son the king."

"Yes," replied the judge's wife; "but that same cat would jump upon the table and shelves, and break my glasses and cups to pieces."

"Oh! there is no fear of *that*!" cried Fritz. "The baker's cat is too polite to do any such thing; and I wish I could walk along the pipes and the roofs of houses as skilfully as he can."

"No cats here, if you please!" cired the judge's wife, who could not bear those domestic animals.

"But, after all," said the judge, who overheard what was going on, "some good may follow from the remarks of Fritz: if you will not have a cat, get a mouse-trap."

"Capital!" cried Fritz: "that idea is very happy, since Godpapa Drosselmayer invented mouse-traps."

Every one now laughed; and as, after a strict search, no such thing as a mouse-trap was found in the house, the servants went to Godfather Drosselmayer, who sent back a famous one, which was baited with a bit of bacon, and placed in the spot where the mice had made such havock.

Mary went to bed with the hope that morning would find the king of the mice a prisoner in the box, to which his gluttony was almost certain to lead him. But at about eleven o'clock, and while she was in her first sleep, she was awoke by something cold and velvety that leapt about her arms and face; and, at the same moment, the whining and squeaking which she knew so well, rang in her ears. The horrible king of the mice was there— seated on her pillow, with his eyes shooting red flames and his seven mouths wide open, as if he were about to eat poor Mary up.

"I laugh at the trap—I laugh at the trap," said the king of the mice: "I shall not go into the little house, and the bacon will not tempt me. I shall not be taken: I laugh at the trap! But you must give me your picture-books and your little silk frock; if not, I will eat up your friend the Nutcracker."

You can very well understand that after such a demand as this, Mary awoke in the morning with her heart full of sorrow and her eyes full of tears. Her mother, moreover, told her nothing new when she said that the trap had remained empty, and that the king of the mice had suspected the snare. Then, as the judge's wife left the room to see after the breakfast, Mary entered her papa's room, and going up to the cupboard, said, "Alas, my dear good Mr. Drosselmayer, where will all this end? When I have given my picture-books to the king of the mice to tear, and my pretty little silk frock, which my guardian angel sent me, to rend into pieces, he will not be content, but will every day be asking me for more. And when I have nothing else left to give him, he will perhaps eat me up in your place. Alas! what can a poor little girl like me do for you, dear good Mr. Drosselmayer? what can I do?"

While Mary was weeping and lamenting in this manner, she observed that the Nutcracker had a drop of blood upon his neck. From the day when she had discovered that her favourite was the son of the toyman and the nephew of the Doctor, she had left off carrying him in her arms, and had neither kissed nor caressed him. Indeed, so great was her timidity in this respect, that she had not even dared to touch him with the tip of her finger.

But at this moment, seeing that he was hurt, and fearing lest his wound might be dangerous, she took him gently out of the cupboard, and began to wipe away with her handkerchief the drop of blood which was upon his neck. But how great was her astonishment, when she suddenly felt the Nutcracker moving about in her hands! She replaced him quickly upon the shelf: his lips quivered from ear to ear, which made his mouth seem larger still; and, by dint of trying to speak, he concluded by uttering the following words: —"Ah, dear Miss Silberhaus—excellent friend—what do I not owe you? and how much gratitude have I to express to you? Do not sacrifice for me your picture-books and your silk frock; but get me a sword—a good sword—and I will take care of the rest!"

The Nutcracker would have said more; but his words became unintelligible—his voice sank altogether—and his eyes, for a moment animated by an expression of the softest melancholy, grew motionless and vacant. Mary felt no alarm: on the contrary, she leapt for joy, for she was very happy at the idea of being able to save the Nutcracker, without being compelled to give up her picture-books or her silk frock. One thing alone vexed her—and that was where could she find the good sword that the little man required? Mary resolved to explain her difficulty to Fritz, who, in spite of his blustering manners, she knew to be a good-natured boy. She accordingly took him up close to the glass cupboard, told him all that had happened between the Nutcracker and the king of the mice, and ended by explaining the nature of the service she required of him. The only thing which made a great impression upon Fritz was the idea that his hussars had really acted in a cowardly manner in the thickest of the battle: he therefore asked Mary if the accusations were really true; and as he knew that she never told a story, he believed her words. Then, rushing up to the cupboard, he made a speech to his soldiers, who seemed quite ashamed of themselves. But this was not all: in order to punish the whole regiment in the person of its officers, he degraded them one after the other, and expressly ordered the band not to play the *Hussar's March* during parade.

Then, turning to Mary, he said, "As for the Nutcracker, who seems to me to be a brave little fellow, I think I can manage his business; for, as I put a veteran major of horse-guards upon half pay yesterday, he having finished his time in the service, I should think he cannot want his sword any longer. It is an excellent blade, I can assure you!"

It now remained to find the major. A search was commenced, and he was found living on his half-pay in a little tavern which stood in a dark corner of the third shelf in the cupboard. As Fritz had imagined, he offered no objection to give up his sword, which had become useless to him, and which was that instant fastened to the Nutcracker's neck.

The fear which Mary now felt prevented her from sleeping all the next night; and she was so wide awake that she heard the clock strike twelve in the room where the cupboard was. Scarcely had the hum of the last stroke ceased, when strange noises came from the direction of the cupboard; and then there was a great clashing of swords, as if two enemies were fighting in mortal combat. Suddenly one of the duellists gave a squeak!

"The king of the mice!" cried Mary, full of joy and terror at the same time.

There was then a dead silence; but presently some one knocked gently—very gently—at the door; and a pretty little voice said, "Dearest Miss Silberhaus, I have glorious news for you: open the door, I beseech you!"

Mary recognized the voice of young Drosselmayer. She hastily put on her little frock, and opened the door. The Nutcracker was there, holding the blood-stained sword

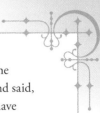

in his right hand and a candle in his left. The moment he saw Mary he knelt down, and said, "It is you alone, O dearest lady! who have nerved me up with the chivalrous courage which I have just shown, and who gave me strength to fight that insolent wretch who dared to threaten you. The vile king of the mice is bathed in his blood. Will you, O lady! deign to accept the trophies of the victory—trophies that are offered by the hand of a knight who is devoted to you until death?"

With these words the Nutcracker drew from his left arm the seven gold crowns of the king of the mice, which he had placed there as if they were bracelets, and which he now offered to Mary, who received them with joy.

The Nutcracker, encouraged by this amiability on her part, then rose and spoke thus: —"Oh! dear Miss Silberhaus, now that I have conquered my enemy, what beautiful things can I show you, if you would have the condescension to go with me only a few paces hence! Oh! do not refuse me—do not refuse me, dear lady—I implore you!"

Mary did not hesitate a moment to follow the Nutcracker, knowing how great were her claims upon his gratitude, and being quite certain that he had no evil intention towards her.

"I will follow you," she said, "my dear Mr. Drosselmayer; but you must not take me very far, nor keep me long away, because I have not yet slept a wink."

"I will choose the shortest, although the most difficult, path," said the Nutcracker; and, thus speaking, he led the way, Mary following him.

The Kingdom of Toys

They both reached, in a short time, a large old cupboard standing in a passage near the door, and which was used as a clothes'-press. There the Nutcracker stopped; and Mary observed, to her great astonishment, that the folding-doors of the cupboard, which were nearly always kept shut, were now wide open, so that she could see plainly her father's travelling-cloak lined with fox-skin, which was hanging over the other clothes. The Nutcracker climbed very skilfully along the border of the cloak; and, clinging to the braiding, he reached the large cape, which, fastened by a piece of lace, fell over the back of the cloak. From beneath this cape the Nutcracker drew down a pretty little ladder of cedar-wood, which he placed in such a manner that the foot touched the bottom of the cupboard, and the top was lost in the sleeve of the cloak.

"Now, dear young lady," said the Nutcracker, "have the goodness to give me your hand and ascend with me."

Mary complied; and scarcely had she glanced up the sleeve, when a brilliant light burst upon her view, and she suddenly found herself transported into the midst of a fragrant meadow, which glittered as if it were strewed with precious stones.

"Oh! how charming!" cried Mary, dazzled by the sight, "where are we?"

"We are in the Field of Sugar-candy, Miss; but we will not remain here, unless you wish to do so. Let us pass through this door."

Then Mary observed a beautiful gate through which they left the field. The gate seemed to be made of white marble, red marble, and blue marble; but when Mary drew near it she saw that it was made of

preserves, candied orange-peel, burnt almonds, and sugared raisins. This was the reason, as she learnt from the Nutcracker, why that gate was called the Gate of Burnt Almonds.

The gate opened into a long gallery, the roof of which was supported by pillars of barley-sugar. In the gallery there were five monkeys, all dressed in red, and playing music, which, if it were not the most melodious in the world, was at least the most original. Mary made so much haste to see more, that she did not even perceive that she was walking upon a pavement of pistachio-nuts and macaroons, which she took for marble. At length she reached the end of the gallery, and scarcely was she in the open air, when she found herself surrounded by the most delicious perfumes, which came from a charming little forest that opened before her. This forest, which would have been dark were it not for the quantity of lamps that it contained, was lighted up in so brilliant a manner that it was easy to distinguish the golden and silver fruits, which were suspended to branches ornamented with white ribands and nosegays, resembling marriage favours.

"Oh! my dear Mr. Drosselmayer," cried Mary, "what is the name of this charming place, I beseech you?"

"We are now in the Forest of Christmas, Miss," answered the Nutcracker; "and it is here that people come to fetch the trees to which the presents sent by the guardian angels are fastened."

"Oh!" continued Mary, "may I not remain here one moment? Everything is so nice here and smells so sweet!"

The Nutcracker clapped his hands together; and several shepherds and shepherdesses, hunters and huntresses, came out of the forest, all so delicate and white that they seemed made of refined sugar. They carried on their shoulders an arm-chair, made of chocolate, incrusted with angelica, in which they placed a cushion of jujube, inviting Mary most politely to sit down. Scarcely had she done so when, as at operas, the shepherds and shepherdesses, the hunters and huntresses, took their places and began to dance a charming ballet to an accompaniment of horns and bugles, which the hunters blew with such good will that their faces became flushed just as if they were made of conserve of roses. Then, the dance being finished, they all disappeared in a grove.

"Pardon me, dear Miss Silberhaus," said the Nutcracker, holding out his hand towards Mary—"pardon me for having exhibited to you so poor a ballet; but those simpletons can do nothing better than repeat, over and over again, the same step. As for the hunters, they blew their bugles as if

they were afraid of them; and I can promise you that I shall not let it pass so quietly. But let us leave those creatures for the present, and continue our walk, if you please."

"I really found it all very delightful," said Mary, accepting the invitation of the Nutcracker; "and it seems to me, my dear Mr. Drosselmayer, that you are harsh towards the little dancers."

The Nutcracker made a face, as much as to say, "We shall see; but your plea in their favour shall be considered." They then continued their journey, and reached a river which seemed to send forth all the sweet scents that perfumed the air.

"This," said the Nutcracker, without even waiting to be questioned by Mary, "is the River of Orange Juice. It is one of the smallest in the kingdom; for, save in respect to its sweet odour, it cannot be compared to the River of Lemonade, which falls into the southern sea, or the Sea of Punch. The Lake of Sweet Whey is also finer: it joins the northern sea, which is called the Sea of Milk of Almonds."

At a short distance was a little village, in which the houses, the church, and the parsonage were all brown; the roofs however were gilt, and the walls were resplendent with incrustations of red, blue, and white sugar-plums.

"This is the Village of Sweet Cake," said the Nutcracker; "it is a pretty little place, as you perceive, and is situate on the Streamlet of Honey. The inhabitants are very agreeable to look upon; but they are always in a bad humour, because they are constantly troubled with the tooth-ache. But, my dear Miss Silberhaus," continued the Nutcracker, "do not let us stop at all the villages and little towns of the kingdom. To the capital! to the capital!"

The Nutcracker advanced, still holding Mary's hand, but walking more confidently than he hitherto had done; for Mary, who was full of curiosity, kept by his side, light as a bird. At length, after the expiration of some minutes, the odour of roses was spread through the air, and everything around them now seemed to be of a rose-tint. Mary remarked that this was the perfume and the reflection of a River of Essence of Roses, which flowed along, its waves rippling melodiously. Upon the sweet-scented waters, silver swans, with collars of gold round their necks, swam gently along, warbling the most delicate songs, so that this harmony, with which they were apparently much pleased, made the diamond fishes leap up around them.

"Ah!" cried Mary, "this is the pretty river which Godpapa Drosselmayer made me at Christmas; and I am the girl who played with the swans!"

THE JOURNEY

The Nutcracker tapped his hands together once more; and, at the moment, the River of Essence of Roses began to rise visibly; and from its swelling waves came forth a chariot made of shells, and covered with precious stones that glittered in the sun. It was drawn by golden dolphins; and four charming little Moors, with caps made of scales of gold-fish and clothes of humming-birds' feathers, leapt upon the bank. They first carried Mary, and then the Nutcracker, very gently down to the chariot, which instantly began to advance upon the stream.

You must confess that it was a ravishing spectacle, and one which might even be compared to the voyage of Cleopatra upon the Cydnus, which you read of in Roman History, to behold little Mary in the chariot of shells, surrounded by perfume, and floating on the waves of essence of roses. The golden dolphins that drew the chariot, tossed up their heads, and threw into the air the glittering jets of rosy crystal, which fell in variegated showers of all the colours of the rainbow. Moreover, that pleasure might penetrate every sense, a soft music began to echo round; and sweet silvery voices were heard singing in the following manner:

> "Who art thou, thus floating where essence of rose
> In a stream of sweet perfume deliciously flows?
> Art thou the Fairies' Queen?
> Say, dear little fishes that gleam in the tide;
> Or answer, ye cygnets that gracefully glide
> Upon that flood serene!"

And all this time the little Moors, who stood behind the seat on the chariot of shells, shook two parasols, hung with bells, in such a manner that those sounds formed an accompaniment to the vocal melody. And Mary, beneath the shade of the parasols, leant over the waters, each wave of which as it passed reflected her smiling countenance.

In this manner she traversed the Riddle of Essence of Roses and reached the bank on the opposite side. Then, when they were within an oar's length of the shore, the little Moors leapt, some into the water, others on the bank, the whole forming a chain so as to convey Mary and

the Nutcracker ashore upon a carpet made of angelica, all covered with mint-drops.

The Nutcracker now conducted Mary through a little grove, which was perhaps prettier than the Christmas Forest, so brilliantly did each tree shine, and so sweetly did they all smell with their own peculiar essence. But what was most remarkable was the quantity of fruits hanging to the branches, those fruits being not only of singular colour and transparency—some yellow as the topaz, others red like the ruby— but also of a wondrous perfume.

"We are now in the Wood of Preserved Fruits," said the Nutcracker, "and beyond that boundary is the capital."

And, as Mary thrust aside the last branches, she was stupefied at beholding the extent, the magnificence, and the novel appearance of the city which rose before her upon a mound of flowers. Not only did the walls and steeples glitter with the most splendid colours, but, in respect to the shape of the buildings, it was impossible to see any so beautiful upon the earth. The fortifications and the gates were built of candied fruits, which shone in the sun with their own gay colours, all rendered more brilliant still by the crystallised sugar that covered them. At the

principal gate, which was the one by which they entered, silver soldiers presented arms to them, and a little man, clad in a dressing-gown of gold brocade, threw himself into the Nutcracker's arms, crying "Oh! dear prince, have you come at length? Welcome—welcome to the City of Candied Fruits!"

Mary was somewhat astonished at the great title given to the Nutcracker; but she was soon drawn from her surprise by the noise of an immense quantity of voices all chattering at the same time; so that she asked the Nutcracker if there were some disturbance or some festival in the Kingdom of Toys?

"There is nothing of all that, dear Miss Silberhaus," answered the Nutcracker; "but the City of Candied Fruits is so happy a place, and all its people are so joyful, that they are constantly talking and laughing. And this is always the same as you see it now. But come with me; let us proceed, I implore of you."

Mary, urged by her own curiosity and by the polite invitation of the Nutcracker, hastened her steps, and soon found herself in a large market-place, which had seen the most magnificent aspects that could possibly be seen. All the houses around were of sugar, open with fretwork, and having balcony over balcony; and in the middle of the market-place was an enormous cake, from the inside of which flowed four fountains, namely, lemonade, orangeade, sweet milk, and gooseberry syrup. The basins around were filled with whipped syllabub, so delicious in appearance, that several well-dressed persons publicly ate of it by means of spoons. But the most agreeable and amusing part of the whole scene, was the crowd of little people who walked about, arm-in-arm, by the thousands and tens of thousands, all laughing, singing, and chattering at the tops of their voices, so that Mary could now account for the joyous din which she had heard. Besides the inhabitants of the capital, there were men of all countries—Armenians, Jews, Greeks, Tyrolese, officers, soldiers, clergymen, monks, shepherds, punches, and all kinds of funny people, such as one meets with in the world.

Presently the tumult redoubled at the entrance of a street looking upon the great square; and the people stood aside to allow the cavalcade to pass. It was the Great Mogul, who was carried upon a palanquin, attended by ninety-three lords of his kingdom and seven hundred slaves: but, at the same time, it happened that from the opposite street the Grand Sultan appeared on horseback, followed by three hundred janissaries. The two sovereigns had always been rivals, and therefore enemies; and this feeling made it impossible for their attendants to meet each other without quarrelling. It was even much worse, as you may well suppose, when those two powerful monarchs found themselves face to face: in the first place there was a great confusion, from the midst of which the citizens sought to save themselves; but cries of fury and despair were soon heard, for a gardener, in the act of running away, had knocked off the head of a Brahmin, greatly respected by his own class; and the Grand Sultan's horse had knocked down a frightened punch, who endeavoured to creep between the animal's legs to get away from the riot. The din was increasing, when the gentleman in the gold brocade dressing-gown, who had saluted the Nutcracker by the title of "Prince" at the gate of the city, leapt to the top of the huge cake with a single bound; and having

run a silvery sweet-toned bell three times, cried out three times, "Confectioner! confectioner! confectioner!"

That instant did the tumult subside and the combatants separate. The Grand Sultan was brushed, for he was covered with dust; the Brahmin's head was fixed on, with the injunction that he must not sneeze for three days, for fear it should fall off again; and order was restored. The pleasant sports began again, and every one hastened to quench his thirst with the lemonade, the orangeade, the sweet milk, or the gooseberry syrup, and to regale himself with the whip-syllabub.

"My dear Mr. Drosselmayer," said Mary, "what is the cause of the influence exercised upon those little folks by the word *confectioner* repeated thrice?"

"I must tell you, Miss," said the Nutcracker, "that the people of the City of Candied Fruits believe, by experience, in the transmigration of souls, and are in the power of a superior principle, called *confectioner*, which principle can bestow on each individual what form he likes by merely baking, for a shorter or longer period, as the case may be. Now, as everyone believes his own existing shape to be the best, he does not like to change it. Hence the magic influence of the word confectioner upon the head of the City of Candied Fruits, when pronounced by the chief magistrate. It is sufficient, as you perceive, to appease all that tumult; everyone in an instant, forgets earthly things, broken ribs, and bumps upon the head; and, restored to himself, says, "*What is man? and what may he not become?*"

While they were thus talking, they reached the entrance of the palace, which shed around a rosy lustre, and was surmounted by a hundred light and elegant towers. The walls were strewed with nosegays, of violets, narcissi, tulips, and jasmine, which set of with their various hues the rose-coloured ground from which they stood forth.

The great dome in the centre was covered with thousands of gold and silver stars.

"O, heavens!" exclaimed Mary, "what is that wonderful building?"

"The Palace of Sweet Cake," answered the Nutcracker; "and it is one of the most famous monuments in the capital of the Kingdom of Toys."

Nevertheless, lost in wonder as she was, Mary could not help observing that the roof of one of the great towers was totally wanting and that the little gingerbread men, mounted on a scaffold of cinnamon, were occupied in repairing it. She was about to question the Nutcracker relative to this accident, when he said, "Alas! It is only a disgrace, if not with absolute ruin. The giant Glutton ate up the top of that tower; and he was already on the point of biting the dome, when the people hastened to give him as a tribute the quarter of the city called Almond and Honey-cake District, together with a large portion of the Forest of Angelica, in consideration of which he agreed to take himself off without making any worse ravages than those which you see."

At that moment a soft and delicious music was heard. The gates of the palace opened themselves, and twelve little pages came forth, carrying in their hands branches of aromatic herbs, lighted like torches. Their heads were made of pearl, six of them had bodies made of rubies, and the six others of emeralds, wherewith they trotted joyously along upon two little feet of gold, sculptured with all the taste and care of Benvenuto Cellini.

They were followed by four ladies, about the same size as Miss Clara, Mary's new doll; but all so splendidly dressed and so richly adorned, that Mary was not at a loss to perceive in them the royal princesses of the City of Preserved Fruits. They all four, upon perceiving the Nutcracker, hastened to embrace him with the utmost tenderness, exclaiming at the same time, and as it were with one voice, "Oh! Prince—dear prince! Dear—dear brother!"

The Nutcracker seemed much moved; he wiped away the tears which flowed from his eyes, and, taking Mary by the hand, said, in a feeling tone, to the four princesses, "My dear sisters, this is Miss Silberhaus whom I now introduce to you. She is the daughter of Chief-Justice Silberhaus, of Nuremberg, a gentleman of the highest respectability. It is this young lady who saved my life; for, if at the moment when I lost a battle she had not thrown her shoe at the king of the mice—and, again, if she had not afterward lent me the sword of a major whom her brother had placed on the half-pay list—I should even now be sleeping in my tomb, or what is worse, be devoured by the king of the mice. "Ah! My dear Miss Silberhaus," cried the Nutcracker, with an enthusiasm which he could not controul, "Pirlipata, although the daughter of a king, was not worthy to unloose the latchet of your pretty little shoes."

"Oh! No—no; certainly not!" repeated the four princesses in chorus; and, throwing their arms round Mary's neck, they cried, "Oh! Noble liberatrix of our dear and much-loved prince and brother! Oh! Excellent Miss Silberhaus!"

And, with these exclamations, which their heart-felt joy cut short, the four princesses conducted the Nutcracker and Mary into the palace, made them sit down upon beautiful little sofas of cedar-wood, covered with golden flowers, and then insisted upon preparing a banquet with their own hands. With this object, they hastened to fetch a number of little vases and bowls made of the finest Japanese porcelain, and silver knives, forks, spoons, and other articles of the table. They then brought in the finest fruits and most delicious sugar-plums that Mary had ever seen, and began to bustle about so nimbly that Mary was at no loss to perceive how well they understood everything connected with cooking. Now, as Mary herself was well acquainted with such matters, she wished inwardly to take a share in all that was going on; and, as if she understood Mary's wishes, the most beautiful of the Nutcracker's four sisters, handed her a little golden mortar, saying, "Dear liberatrix of my brother, pound me some sugar-candy, if you please."

Mary hastened to do as she was asked; and while she was pounding the sugar-candy in the mortar, when a delicious music came forth, the Nutcracker began to relate all his adventures: but, strange as it was, it seemed to Mary during that recital, as if the words of young Drosselmayer and the noise of the pestle came gradually more and more indistinct to her ears. In a short time she seemed to be surrounded by a light vapour turned into a silvery mist, which spread more and more densely around her, so that it presently concealed the Nutcracker and the princesses from her sight. Strange songs, which reminded her of those she had heard on the River of Essence of Roses, met her ears, commingled with the increasing murmur of waters; and then Mary thought that the waves flowed beneath her, raising her up in their swell. She felt as if she were rising high up—higher—and higher; when, suddenly, down she fell from a precipice that she could not measure.

Conclusion

One does not fall several thousand feet without awaking. Thus it was that Mary awoke; and, on awaking, she found herself in her little bed. It was broad daylight, and her mother, who was standing by her, said, "Is it possible to be so lazy as you are?

Come, get up, and dress yourself, dear little Mary, for breakfast is waiting."

"Oh! my dear mamma," said Mary, opening her eyes wide with astonishment, "whither did young Mr. Drosselmayer take me last night? And what splendid things did he show me?"

Then Mary related all that I have just told you; and when she had done her mother said, "You have had a very long and charming dream, dear little Mary; but now that you are awake, you must forget it all, and come and have your breakfast."

But Mary, while she dressed herself, persisted in maintaining that she had really seen all she spoke of. Her mother accordingly went to the cupboard and took out the Nutcracker, who, according to custom, was upon the third shelf. Bringing it to her daughter, she said, "How can you suppose, silly child, that this puppet, which is made of wood and cloth, can be alive, or move, or think?"

But, my dear mamma," said Mary, perpetually, I am well aware that the Nutcracker is none other than young Mr. Drosselmayer, the nephew of godpapa."

At that moment Mary heard a loud shout of laughter behind her.

It was the judge, Fritz, and Miss Trudchen, who made themselves merry at her expense.

"Ah!" cried Mary, "how can you laugh at me, dear papa, and at my poor Nutcracker? He spoke very respectfully of you, nevertheless, when we went to the Palace of Sweet Cake, and he introduced me to his sisters."

The shouts of laughter redoubled to such an extent that Mary began to see the necessity of giving some proof of the truth of what she said, for fear of being treated as a simpleton. She therefore went into the adjoining room and brought back a little box in which she had carefully placed the seven crowns of the king of the mice.

"Here, mamma," she said, "are the seven crowns of the king of the mice, which the Nutcracker gave me last night as a proof of his victory."

The judge's wife, full of surprise, took the seven little crowns, which were made of an unknown but very brilliant metal, and were carved with a delicacy of which human hands were incapable. The judge himself could not take his eyes off them, and considered them to be so precious, that, in spite of the prayers of Fritz, he would not let him touch one of them.

The judge and his wife then pressed Mary to tell them whence came those little crowns; but she could only persist in what she had said already: and when her father, annoyed at what he heard and at what he considered obstinacy on her part, called her a little "story-teller," she burst into tears, exclaiming, "Alas! unfortunate child that I am! What would you have me tell you?"

At that moment the door opened, and the doctor made his appearance.

"What is the matter?" he said, "and what have they done to my little god-daughter that she cries and sobs like this? What is it? what is it all?"

The judge acquainted Doctor Drosselmayer with all that had occurred; and, when the story was ended, he showed him the seven crowns. But scarcely had the doctor seen them, when he burst out laughing, and said, "Well, really this is too good! These are the seven crowns that I used to wear to my watch-chain some years ago, and which I gave to my goddaughter on the occasion of her second birthday. Do you not remember, my dear friend?"

But the judge and his wife could not recollect anything about the present stated to have been given. Nevertheless, believing what the godfather said, their countenances became more calm. Mary, upon seeing this, ran up to Doctor Drosselmayer, saying, "But you know all, godpapa! confess that the Nutcracker is your nephew, and that it was he who gave me the seven crowns."

But Godfather Drosselmayer did not at all seem to like these words; and his face became so gloomy, that the judge called little Mary to him, and taking her upon his knees, said "Listen to me, my dear child, for I wish to speak to you very seriously. Do me the pleasure, once for all, to put an end to these silly ideas; because, if you should again assert that this ugly and deformed Nutcracker is the nephew of our friend the doctor, I give you due warning that I will throw, not only the Nutcracker, but all the other toys, Miss Clara amongst them, out of the window."

Poor Mary was therefore unable to speak any more of all the fine things with which her imagination was filled but you can well understand that when a person has once travelled in such a fine place as the Kingdom of Toys, and seen such a delicious town as the City of Preserved Fruits, were it only for an hour, it is not easy to forget such sights.

Mary therefore endeavoured to speak of her brother of the whole business; but she had lost all of his confidence since the moment when she had said that his hussars had taken to flight. Convinced, therefore, that Mary was a story-

teller, as her father had said so, he restored his
officers to the rank from which he had reduced
them, and allowed the band to play as usual
the *Hussar's March*—a step which did not
prevent Mary from entertaining her
own opinion relative to their courage.

Many dared not therefore speak
further of her adventures. Nevertheless,
the remembrance of the Kingdom of
Toys followed her without ceasing;
and when she thought of all that, she
looked upon it as it she were still in the Christmas Forest, or on the River
of Essence of Roses, or in the City of Preserved Fruits; —so that, instead
of playing with her toys as she had been wont to do, she remained silent
and pensive, occupied only with her own thoughts, while every one called
her "the little dreamer."

But one day, when the doctor, with his wig laid upon the ground,
his tongue thrust into one corner of his mouth, and the sleeves of his
yellow coat turned up, was mending a clock by the aid of a long pointed
instrument, it happened that Mary, who was seated near the glass
cupboard contemplating the Nutcracker, and buried in her own thoughts,
suddenly said, quite forgetful that both the doctor and her mamma were
close by, "Ah! my dear Mr. Drosselmayer, if you were not a little man
made of wood, as my papa declares, and if you really were alive, I would
not do as Princess Pirlipata did, and desert you because, in serving me,
you had ceased to be a handsome young man; for I love you sincerely!"

But scarcely had she uttered these words, when there was such a noise
in the room, that Mary fell off her chair in a fainting fit.

When she came to herself, she found that she was in the arms of her
mother, who said, "How is it possible that a great girl like you, I ask,

can be so foolish as to fall off your chair—and just at the moment, too, when young Mr. Drosselmayer, who has finished his travels, arrives at Nuremberg? Come, wipe your eyes, and be a good girl."

Indeed, as Mary wiped her eyes, the door opened and Godpapa Drosselmayer, with his glass wig upon his head, his hat under his arm, and his drab frock-coat upon his back, entered the room. He wore a smiling countenance, and held by the hand a young man, who, although very little, was handsome. This young man wore a superb frock-coat of red velvet embroidered with gold, white silk stockings, and shoes brilliantly polished. He had a charming nosegay on the bosom of his shirt, and was very dandified with his curls and hair-powder; moreover, long tresses, neatly braided, hung behind his back. The little sword that he wore by his side was brilliant with precious stones; and the hat which he carried under his arm was of the finest silk.

The amiable manners of this young man showed who he was directly; for scarcely had he entered the room, when he placed at Mary's feet a quantity of magnificent toys and nice confectionary—chiefly sweet cake and sugar-plum, the finest she had ever tasted, save in the Kingdom of Toys. As for Fritz, the doctor's nephew seemed to have guessed his martial taste, for he brought him a sword with a blade of the finest Damascus steel. At table, when the dessert was placed upon it, the amiable youth cracked nuts for all the company: the hardest could not resist his teeth for a moment. He

placed them in his mouth with his right hand; with the left he pulled his hair behind; and, crack! the shell was broken.

Mary had become very red when she first saw that pretty little gentleman; but she blushed deeper still, when, after the dessert, he invited her to go with him into the room where the glass cupboard was.

"Yes, go my dear children, and amuse yourselves together," said Godpapa Drosselmayer: "I do not want that room any more to-day, since all the clocks of my friend the judge now go well."

The two young people proceeded to the room; but scarcely was young Drosselmayer alone with Mary, when he fell upon one knee, and spoke thus:

"My dear Miss Silberhaus, you see at your feet the happy Nathaniel Drosselmayer, whose life you saved on this very spot. You also said that you would not have repulsed me, as Princess Pirlipata did, if, in serving *you*, I had become hideous. Now, as the spell which the queen of the mice threw upon me was destined to lose all its power on that day when, in spite of my ugly face, I should be beloved by a young and beautiful girl, I at that moment ceased to be a vile Nutcracker and resumed my proper shape, which is not disagreeable, as you may see. Therefore, my dear young lady, if you still possess the same sentiments in respect to myself, do me the favour to bestow your much-loved hand upon me, share my throne and my crown, and reign with me over the Kingdom of Toys, of which I ere now become the king."

Then Mary raised young Drosselmayer gently, and said "You are an amiable and a good king, sir; and as you have moreover a charming kingdom, adorned with magnificent palaces, and possessing a very happy people, I receive you as my future husband, provided my parents give their consent."

Thereupon, as the door of the room had opened very gently without the two young folks having heard it, so occupied were they with their own sentiments, the judge, his wife, and Godpapa Drosselmayer came forward, crying "Bravo!" with all their might; which made Mary as red as a cherry. But the young man was not abashed; and, advancing towards the judge and his wife, he bowed gracefully to them, paid them a handsome compliment, and ended by soliciting the hand of Mary in marriage. The request was immediately granted.

That same day Mary was engaged to Nathaniel Drosselmayer, on condition that the marriage should not take place for a year.

At the expiration of the year, the bridegroom came to fetch the bride in a little carriage of mother of pearl incrusted with gold and silver, and drawn by ponies of the size of sheep, but which were of countless worth, because there were none like them in the world. The young king took his bride to the Palace of Sweet cake, where they were married by the chaplain. Twenty-two thousand little people, all covered with pearls, diamonds, and brilliant stones, danced at the bridal.

Even at the present day, Mary is still queen of that beautiful country, where may be seen brilliant forests of Christmas; rivers of orangeade, sweet milk, and essence of roses; transparent palaces of sugar whiter than snow and cleaner than ice; —in a word, all kinds of wonderful and extraordinary things may there be seen by those who have eyes sharp enough to discover them.

ABOUT THE AUTHORS

E(rnst) T(heodor) A(madeus) Hoffmann was born in 1776 in
Königsberg (now part of Russia), where he lived until 1796. After
studying to be a lawyer, he took a job as a civil servant in the Prussian
government and held postings in Poland and Germany. In his spare
time, Hoffmann wrote music and fiction, publishing his first story in
1809. His first two story collections, whose titles translate as *Fantasy
Pieces*, appeared in 1814 and established him as a leading writer in the
German romantic fantasy tradition. They were followed by the novels
The Devil's Elixirs (1815–1816) and *The Life and Opinions of the Tomcat
Murr* (1819–1821), and two more collections of tales, *Night Pieces*
(1815–1817) and *The Serapion Brothers* (1819–1822). His opera *Undine*
was produced in 1816. Hoffmann died in Berlin in 1822.

Alexandre Dumas was born in Villers-Cotterets, on the outskirts of
Paris, in 1802. Well-read in his youth, Dumas began writing for the
stage in 1825 and published his first novel in 1838. His swashbuckling
historical romances, which include *The Three Musketeers* (1844), *The
Count of Monte Cristo* (1844–1845), and *The Man in the Iron Mask*
(1847–1850), proved popular with international audiences and established
him as one of the bestselling authors of the nineteenth century. At the
time of his death in 1870, he had published more than 250 books and
was among France's best-loved writers.